DRAGON PROTECTOR

DRAGON DREAMS 1

LEELA ASH

TABITHA ST. GEORGE

Dragon Protector

Join the Totally Romance Facebook Group!

https://www.totallyromancebooks.com/leela-ash

CONTENTS

$\mathcal{G}$olden and mysterious, the coin in Hannah Stiles' hand hinted that there was hope. That, maybe, just maybe, there was a path out of this disaster.

From downstairs, she caught snatches of her parents' hushed debate.

"...extremely generous offer... we won't see another like it..."

"...but we'll lose everything!"

"Everything except our son."

Silence fell. There was no arguing against that last point. Four months ago, a hit and run driver struck her seventeen-year-old brother Danny as he walked home one evening. Bills mounted. Insurance, that had promised the world, delivered far less protection than they needed. Hannah didn't know the details. Even though she was six years older than her brother, her parents still treated her like their little princess. They tried to shield her from life's ugly truths.

But things had come to a head and there was no hiding now. Her parents owed the hospital $72,300. As much as their small farm made in an entire year! With their savings drained, a 'savior' had appeared, a real estate developer who made them a very generous offer for their farm. Enough money to cover their debts and set up somewhere else...

...if they were willing to abandon their home. A house that had been in the Stiles' family for centuries. The place where she and her father had grown up. Her parents hated the idea – but there was no other option.

Except this coin.

Hannah took a deep, shaky breath and prayed it was as magical as Grandpa had said. "When things are darkest," he'd told her, "when there's no hope at all, show this to the Protectors. They are bound by blood and honor to aid us."

Unfortunately, he hadn't told her how to find those 'Protectors'. *His* grandfather hadn't bothered to pass that important detail along. Being a modern girl, Hannah didn't believe in ancient debts and magic coins. But if this thing had truly been in her family for 300 years, it must be valuable. Maybe valuable enough to save their home. And she had a good idea where to find a 'Protector' of her own.

Online.

A quick image search didn't turn up anything that looked similar. The coin itself didn't offer many clues about its origin. No date, no sign of what country it came from. One side was blank. On the other, a dragon curled around the edge, circling two words: *"Noraste Mel."* Google couldn't translate that. When she posted on a rare coins forum, no one had ever heard of anything like it.

Until yesterday, when an email arrived:

Ms. Stiles,

I am keenly interested in the coin you describe. If I am right about its origins, it is priceless. Though, surely, its Protector has told you that?

I need to see the coin to be certain. I will arrange a video conference tomorrow night at 6:00. Do have the coin with you.
    Sincerely,
    Brandon Lorde

TWO WORDS SENT BUTTERFLIES WINGING THROUGH HER stomach. 'Priceless' – because that could save them. And 'Protector' – a strange echo of her grandpa's own words. Quickly, she'd agreed to speak to Mr. Lorde tonight.

Her computer's clock read 5:58pm. Hannah set the coin down and ran a hand through her long blonde hair. Nervously, she swept a wrinkle out of her sleeve and worried that perhaps jeans and a faded state fair t-shirt weren't the best choice to impress a stranger.

Nonsense, she scolded herself. *This isn't a date. He's interested in your coin, not you.*

The exact moment the clock ticked over to 6:00pm, a soft ping announced that Mr. Lorde wished to begin a video chat.

Hannah licked her lips and clicked 'accept'.

She had expected some little old man surrounded by cats, coins, and dusty antiques. Instead, a Greek god appeared on her screen.

Black hair, thick and light as a raven's wings, framed his strong, angular face. Everything about him radiated strength, from his muscular arms to the sharp cut of his jaw and his full, firm lips. And his eyes...!

They caught her and held her as tightly as a hare in a hawk's grasp. She had never seen eyes like them before. Rich, sapphire blue. For a moment, she swore there were lights in them, tiny flecks of purest gold that swirled around the pupils' dark center.

Hannah's breath caught in her throat. She simply stared,

like a deer in headlights, wishing, once again, that she'd changed clothes after coming in from the barn.

For a moment, those luscious, mesmerizing eyes scanned her, drinking in every detail of her face, her clothes, her hair. Perhaps it was crazy, but he seemed… eager? Anxious? No, nothing that weak. But clearly, whatever this coin was, it held great importance to him.

"Ms. Stiles?"

Even his voice thrilled her, a deep, rich bass that transformed her plain, boring name into something enchanting.

He cleared his throat. "Ms. Stiles?"

Oh heavens! He expected an answer? Blood rushed to Hannah's cheeks as she realized she'd been sitting there staring at him. "Yes? Uh, yes! I'm, uh, Hannah. Hannah Stiles."

"Good. Please hold the coin up to your computer's camera."

No small talk? No 'Hi, how are you, nice to see you?' For the first time, she felt a twinge of uneasiness, but she ignored it. Of course, he was all business. A wealthy, elegant man like him would never care about a plain farm girl like her. Still blushing, she raised the coin, so he could see it.

Immediately, he gasped. Some bright emotion lit his azure eyes. Hope? Joy? She couldn't tell. For one moment, a dazzled smile brightened his face and he began to speak in a deep, musical language.

What it was, she had no idea. Certainly nothing like her high school Spanish. He fell silent, awaiting an answer. Hannah winced. "I'm sorry. I don't know that language."

At once, clouds of suspicion darkened his handsome face. He repeated the last sentence, his smile fading.

"Sorry, I really don't have any idea what you're saying."

"*Marakeen?*" Those brilliant eyes bored into her now, seeking traps and deceit. "This word means nothing to you?"

Hannah shook her head. "Is that the name of the coin?"

His eyes closed, freeing her. Every muscle in his lithe body tensed, as if some fierce battle raged inside him. When he opened his eyes again, they were as cold as glacial ice. Chin raised, he stared through the computer at her with chilly disdain. "So, tell me, where did you steal the coin from?"

Steal?!? Now *her* eyes flashed. "Excuse me? How dare you accuse me of theft?"

"How dare I?" he sneered. "You have no idea what you hold in your hand. Clearly, you are a thief."

"This coin has been in my family for hundreds of years!"

"And yet, you know nothing of the *Marakeen?*" She glared back at him, unwilling to answer, and he gave a short bark of laughter. "Then let me correct myself. You are not a thief – you are the descendent of thieves."

"I think this conversation is over," Hannah hissed. Gorgeous or not, he didn't get to sit there and insult her family like that.

As she reached for the mouse, his lip curled in mockery. "Don't you want your money, thief's child?"

Hannah froze, and now it was her turn to fight back anger.

Money. That was why she was here. She couldn't forget that. Couldn't let her anger... her disappointment, cloud her mind. Yes, her 'Greek god' seemed to be more of a devil. Yes, he was arrogant, and dismissive, and...

She swallowed and scrubbed her eyes, quickly wiping away any trace of the shamed tears his taunts had summoned. None of that mattered. What mattered was that, judging from the luxurious furniture she saw behind him, he was rich. And he wanted her coin.

"Well?"

His scornful gaze burned through her, hitting her soul like a hammer's blow. Yet she forced herself to meet it. To lift her chin and defy his unjust accusations. "Yes. $72,300. That's what this coin will cost you."

He didn't even blink at that crazy price tag. "An oddly specific price."

She held her tongue. He didn't deserve an explanation.

"Very well." Clearly, his interest in the subject had died. "$72,300 it is. I will mail you my address. Send the coin to me and I will give you what you want."

"I want the money first!" Her lips pinched. "I don't trust you."

"Well, *I* don't trust thieves," he countered, "and I have the money. You will not be paid until the coin is in my possession."

As she opened her mouth to argue, he waved dismissively. "We're done here," he said, as the video conference ended.

For a moment, Hannah sat there, shaking with shame and rage. How could someone so heavenly, so gorgeous, be so cruel? What had she done to deserve that kind of treatment?

By all rights, she ought to be dancing with joy. She'd done it! She'd found the money her family needed to save their land! But all she could think about was his eyes, and the way the hope and joy they held had died. She hadn't done a thing wrong, and yet here she sat, feeling vaguely guilty. Sure that, somehow, she'd disappointed this stranger.

Rude stranger, she reminded herself. He was in the wrong, not her.

A ping announced the arrival of his address. New York City – not so far from her upstate home.

She stared at it until her mother's voice called her to dinner. And when she rose, she had a plan.

Mr. Brandon Lorde of New York City would get his coin alright.

But not the way he expected.

CHAPTER 2

A day later, Brandon Lorde was still stewing about that treacherous thief as he jogged through Central Park.

Normally, he drew attention on his runs. His dark charisma, as well as his relentless pace, caught the eyes of everyone he passed. By the time sweat plastered his shirt to the hard lines of his muscled body, he would turn the head of any woman in the park.

Not today. Today, a fierce anger burned inside him. Nothing was worse than a thief, a person who stole what another had claimed. Humans and animals both despised anything that took what was not theirs.

Their displeasure was a pale shadow of his own fury. For, while he looked like a perfectly sculpted human man, he was much, much more. He was a Dragon Shifter, a *Marakeen* in the Old Tongue. An ancient guardian who resided half in this world, half in the Other Side. To mortal eyes, he was nothing more than a strikingly handsome man. Only those with Shifter blood could see the majestic Dragon of his soul.

Once his breed had been guardians, protectors of the

Wellsprings that brought magic and life from the Other Side to this world. But Earth had turned from magic. The Wellsprings dried up, tearing a hole in the souls of all Dragonkind. They were Guardians of Nothing. Protectors of the Past. No matter how much wealth they gathered and hoarded, no pleasure ever filled that gaping rift.

Yesterday, for one exhilarating, terrible moment, he had dared to dream of finding his purpose at long last. Hannah Stiles' 'coin' was a piece of Blood Gold, the token that a Dragon gave to someone who saved his life. He, and all Dragons, owed its owner a debt of honor. A debt that honor demanded be repaid, even at the cost of the Dragon's life.

And when he had seen the girl...

Purity and sweetness. She didn't need any of the fancy clothes and expensive jewelry city women piled upon themselves. Her beauty came from within. The sweep of her silken hair, the way it spilled around her shoulders. The warmth that lit her brown eyes when she smiled. The swell of her breasts under the plain clothes she wore, hinting that a woman's full lusciousness lay beneath that innocent gaze.

His first thought had been, here is someone worthy. Someone he could devote his life to protecting. It would be his honor, his joy to repay whatever debt was owed her.

Of course, that all turned out to be a lie. *Again.* Three times now, con artists had tried to fool him with stolen Blood Gold. Each scam breathed life into his dying dream, the prayer that, someday, he would find a person worthy of service. Someone he could live for – and die for, if necessary.

Well, not today. He could not fall for this trick again! Brandon gritted his teeth as another flare of anger surged up from his Dragon. A passing dog walker couldn't sense that. But the three pugs she led flinched away from him, yelping. Animals had much keener senses than their human masters.

Brandon struggled to calm his Dragon; the dogs didn't

deserve even a brush with a Dragon's wrath. It retreated, still brooding over the shock of finding that this Hannah wasn't as pure as she seemed.

Disappointing. He sighed. But the world was full of disappointments. Some days it seemed like that was all that was left now that the Wellsprings had run dry.

One last block brought him home to his brownstone. As he stepped through the front door onto the silver marble foyer, he sensed a disturbance. Someone was here. Someone… strangely familiar.

Amarie, the elderly Witch-Hare who minded his home, stepped out of the kitchen carrying a tea tray. "You have a guest, Master," she said, confirming his suspicion.

He frowned. "I wasn't expecting anyone."

The housekeeper swept past him. "She *is* expected, though."

His frown deepened. "By whom?"

Amarie paused in the sitting room doorway and glanced at him with her odd, mismatched eyes. One blue, one green. "How should I know? I'm just a 'crazy Witch-Hare.' But she *is* expected." Then she breezed past, as if her words made sense.

As mad as Hares often seemed, the years had taught him that an eerie prescience often lurked beneath his housekeeper's "nonsense." He drifted after her, curious what the waters of Fate had washed to his shore.

He stepped into the parlor and, at once, his gaze was drawn to the bay window. There, amidst velvet cushions, sat a vision.

The girl.

In the late afternoon light, her hair burned as bright as honey in the sun. Gold and warm, a gentle mirror of the blazing scales of his own soul. She was taller than he imagined, with the willowy grace of a gazelle. Her shyness might seem weak to some. But as she saw him, a quiet strength firmed her features. A hint, perhaps, that true steel lay somewhere beneath her mild demeanor. He wondered if life had ever forced her to find her own power.

Suddenly, that question meant the world to him. He wanted to sit beside her, arm brushing against her sweet curves, and ask…

NO!

His Dragon's anger shattered that pleasant image. This was not some innocent maiden, his Shifter soul warned. She was a thief.

Once again, he felt the bitter sting of disappointment. But his Dragon was right. He had to stay on his guard.

"Ms. Stiles." He strode over to the table and took a cup of tea from Amarie. "I told you to mail the coin to me." His Dragon still seethed, and he allowed the faintest touch of its displeasure to warm his tone. He was the Alpha of his Flight, and not accustomed to being disobeyed.

She flinched, as if she could feel his Dragon's hot annoyance. Yet, she rose to her feet, tall and proud, and faced him. "I chose not to. You gave me no reason to trust you."

She dared hint that *he* was untrustworthy? A few short, angry steps brought him to his writing desk. He turned his back on her beautiful, impudent face and found his checkbook. "As you will. The price we agreed upon was $72,000, yes?"

"No. $72,300."

Again, the exactness of that amount puzzled him. "$73,000 then."

"No." Her denial was soft, but implacable. "$72,300."

"You don't want an extra $700?" What kind of thief would turn down more?

She shook her head, sending a ripple of sunlight shimmering across her long hair. "I only need $72,300."

"But why refuse the extra money?" he pressed.

"Because I don't want to owe you. I wouldn't take any of your money if I wasn't desperate."

Shock froze his tongue. Even his Dragon subsided, confused. For the first time, Brandon wondered if he had made a terrible mistake. If he had misjudged her... offered insult to an innocent person...

He opened his mouth to say that, but the words caught in his throat. He was an Alpha. A Dragon. Lord of his Flight. Admitting mistakes did not come naturally to him. And yet...

And yet, Truth was more valuable than Pride. Any honorable Shifter – any honorable man – knew this. If he had made a mistake, he would correct it.

He coughed to cover his disquiet. Amarie finished unloading her tea tray and scurried off, leaving the two of them alone. Awkward silence fell in her wake.

Something had to be said. "Why are you desperate?" he asked at last. A hint of a growl frosted the words. Immediately, her eyes narrowed, and he hurried to cut off her outburst. "I understand that I have no right to ask this." To his relief, her anger dimmed. *She had a forgiving soul*, he thought, *if it took so little to placate her.* "But I am curious why anyone would sell a family heirloom."

"Because family is more important than any antique," she replied, "and if I have to choose between the two, my family comes first."

As it should. That was a noble answer.

Not at all the answer of a thief. It seemed ever more likely that he had erred. In response, his Dragon went completely silent. Apparently, apologies were his business, not the Dragon's.

"Would you tell me why your family needs precisely $72,300? Please," he added, as she hesitated.

"My brother was hit by a car four months ago, just before he graduated from high school. They never caught the driver. My parents own a small farm, north of Albany. We had insurance," she sighed, "but…"

"It failed to cover expenses? By $72,300?"

She nodded. The last traces of her anger faded, swept away by a tired grief. "I don't want to sell this coin. My grandpa loved it, and it's been in my family for centuries."

The conversation had circled round to the question that still bothered him. How was that possible? She could be Kindred, a descendent of some ancient Shifter. But how could she hold Blood Gold in her hand and know nothing about the *Marakeen*, the Dragons who made such things? Had knowledge of the Other Side truly faded so much in the years since the Wellsprings died?

Wait. North of Albany? Brandon owned old diaries, written in the days when New York was still New Amsterdam, which claimed that a Wellspring lay in *"Beverwyck."* That was the general term the Dutch used to describe much of their northern colony. Could that lie somewhere on Hannah's farm?

But her name… "New York was originally a Dutch colony. Surely 'Stiles' isn't a Dutch name?"

Now he'd annoyed her again. She folded her arms across her chest. "We used to be Vanstiles."

He paused, letting that sink in. She was Kindred, then. One of her ancestors truly had saved a Dragon's life.

And he had offered her insult for it, rather than repaying the debt with joy and honor, as he should have done. An acid curl of shame twisted his guts.

Hannah watched him, wary and defensive.

He'd done that. She'd come to him with innocent hope and he had thrown disdain back in her face.

There was only one thing to do then. "I believe you," he assured her. Again, she relaxed quickly, and he thanked the stars for her kind nature. "I also owe you an apology. I should not have called you a thief. I jumped to conclusions. I..." He swallowed and waited to see if his Dragon would object, but the Great Serpent was completely silent. "I am sorry for that."

"Okay." Maybe it wasn't an enthusiastic acceptance, yet her arms dropped to her sides. "But why? Why did you think I had to be a thief?"

What could he say to that? Shifter law demanded that the affairs of the Changing Kind remain hidden from mortals. Technically, she was – probably – Kindred. That made her exempt from the rule. But if her family remembered nothing of their Shifter heritage, weren't they essentially humans? Could he reveal the secrets of his Flight to someone who knew nothing of Shifters?

Would she even believe him?

No, of course not. The moment he spoke of Dragons and Blood Debts, she'd decide he was crazy. He couldn't bear that. Better to have her think him a jerk than a madman.

"It's… a long story. And foolish." She waited. He shook his head. "Something I would rather not discuss, if it is all the same to you."

Hannah's nose wrinkled, a subtle sign that no, that was not enough to completely satisfy her. But it would have to do.

"I think I can offer you something much more satisfying than words, however. Here." Quickly, he wrote a check for the money she needed. He held it out to her, but when she took it, he kept his grip on the paper. Binding the two of them together for one brief moment.

"Hannah Stiles, Daughter of Kindred not known to me, I stand before you."

She blinked at the odd, formal lilt of his words. Brandon didn't care. Few things held more honor than the repayment of a Blood Debt. Neither he nor his Dragon could rob this moment of the ceremony it deserved. Even if the woman he repaid had no clue what that debt, or his words, meant.

"I, Brandon, Lord of the First Flight, thank you for the gift your family gave my Kind. I will assume the debt and repay it, though it cost me my life's blood."

At that, she bit her lip. He longed to dispel her nervousness with a soft kiss. But he didn't dare touch her, lest he frighten her. Instead, he pressed on.

"You have asked me for money. $72,300. That, I give you freely. Know, however, that I do not believe this money satisfies the debt owed to you.

"I swear, on my soul and my honor, that I will protect your family from this tragedy. I give you this money now." He released the check. He half expected her to flinch away from him and his strange speech. Instead, she stood still, frozen, watching him with a curious mixture of puzzlement, relief...

And hope. That warmed him, to the bottom of his soul.

"If any other expenses arise, speak to me and I will pay them, whatever they may be." A soft gasp of happiness escaped her lips and the urge to pull her close grew stronger. "If you need anything – money, help, support – you need only tell me. I will take care of it. And of you."

For a moment, Hannah stood silently, unsteady from the shock of his offer. Brandon took her shoulder in his hand, steadying her with a gentle but unshakeable strength. She leaned toward him, as if drawn, and her full, sensuous lips part. He bowed his head toward her and...

The parlor door thumped open. "Right!" Amarie barked.

Hannah and Brandon jumped apart like a pair of startled cats, then stared at the old woman.

The housekeeper seemed oblivious to the moment she'd ruined. "I've taken the lady's bag, such as it was, smallish thing!"

"What?" The girl stared at her, baffled. "Why would you take my things?"

"Well, I haven't taken-them, taken-them," Amarie insisted. "If you know what I mean. I've just taken them up to your room."

Hannah's confusion deepened. "My room? But I'm not staying the night."

"Do you have a hotel?" Brandon asked. "I can call a cab for you if you wish."

That surprised a breathy laugh from her. "No, I couldn't afford a New York hotel. I'm going to drive straight home."

He frowned. "But it's almost dark already. Better to drive in the morning, when you're rested."

"Oh, if I get tired, I'll just pull over and sleep in the car."

Now his Dragon roused itself again, having vanished for the apology. It grumbled, deeply dissatisfied with the idea of this young lady sleeping alone, unprotected, in a car on the side of the road.

Brandon didn't need any prompting. "Nonsense. My guest bedroom is far safer – and *far* more comfortable. Stay the night. You can leave in the morning."

When she hesitated, he added, "Please?"

Once again, that word worked miracles. A shy smile lit her face and she nodded. "Well, okay, I guess... yes, that would be nice."

"Wonderful. Allow me to offer you a proper dinner. It's the least I can do to apologize for calling you a thief. Amarie, would you..."

"Already have," the Witch-Hare chirped, as she primly marched off to the kitchen.

CHAPTER 3

That night, sleep came slowly to Hannah. Despite the sultry sleekness of the bed's Egyptian cotton sheets, she tossed and turned. Exhausted, drained, her mind still raced over the day's events and the wild swings of Fate.

How could a man change so much in a blink of an eye? Yesterday, he branded her a thief. Today – for no reason she could see – he took that word back and pledged to protect her family. What happened? What had she done?

Round and round her mind twisted, finding no answers. None added up. Not Brandon's unexpected kindness. Not the splendid seven-course meal his housekeeper somehow whipped together. Not his pledge of unconditional support.

The worst thing? She wasn't sure she cared that it didn't make sense.

Who needed "sense" when a millionaire promised to banish all her problems? Was "sense" more important than his rapt, vibrant eyes studying her over a glass of champagne? Than the fact that he seemed to find her more intoxicating than the finest wines? Her! Hannah Stiles, a farmer's daughter. A woman who didn't know the difference between a "shiraz" and a... a... whatever that other wine was.

She'd been so embarrassed to admit that she knew nothing about wine. Surely, he'd find that crude, unsophisticated. Instead, he simply smiled and said, "Then I have so many wonderful things to introduce to you."

No. Sense was worthless next to that. She didn't know why, but the Greek god she'd dreamed of was back.

And about to vanish.

That was the worm hidden in the apple. None of this could last.

Tomorrow, she would wake up. She'd shower, have breakfast. Probably a lovely one, knowing how Amarie cooked. And then? Nothing. A polite goodbye. A handshake. Then she would go home to her family. He would stay here, in his New York mansion. They would never see each other again. The magic of this fairy-tale evening would vanish like a soap bubble.

Facing that, how could she sleep? Basking in the glow of his laughter, his smiles... and knowing she'd never possess them again.

Rest seemed impossible. The body, however, can't be denied forever. Somewhere past midnight, her fatigue finally silenced her feverish mind and dragged her down into sleep.

IN THE DREAM, SHE STOOD IN A SMALL CLEARING. YOUNG birch trees surrounded it, whispering softly in the night breeze. A full moon rode high overhead, bathing everything in its gentle, silver glow. At the heart of the glade, a pool glittered. Its waters sent wisps of light, like tiny bubbles, sailing up to the night sky.

Hannah barely noticed it, because *he* was there. Brandon.

He stood before her, barefoot on the mossy ground. Only

a thin silken robe hid his lean, powerful form from her hungry eyes. It left his chest bare and heat flared deep inside her as her gaze traveled slowly down his taut muscles. Strong, fully masculine, his body held not an ounce of softness – and her own body came alive in its presence. A light sash pulled the robe closed around his hips, teasing her. Taunting her to imagine what hard, male delight waited below.

Her own clothes reflected Brandon's, green silk to his gold. A gentle breeze swirled around her, sending silken folds whispering across her skin like a lover's kiss. Hannah's breath grew ragged. She wanted him. She needed him. And why shouldn't she offer herself to him? It was just a dream, after all.

A cold dart of fear struck her heart at that thought. She's ruined it! Dreams vanished as soon as you recognized what they were. Hannah flinched, sure she would wake in her bed drenched in sweat. Aching at the loss. To see him, nearly naked, in all his male glory... and to have that vision ripped from her before she could taste his wonders...

But the dream remained. Joy filled her, twining with her desire and delight as she realized that no, this time, Fate wouldn't rob her. For one night, in one dream, he was hers.

Brandon stepped toward her, ready to claim her, to explore the wonders of her own soft, feminine form.

With a flicker, however, the dream shifted. She now held a cup in her hands. A silver chalice filled with the glittering waters of the glade's pool. In his right hand, a golden dagger appeared, curved like the fang of some great serpent. Both of them hesitated. As they did, distant thunder growled across the sky. Words were hidden in its rumbles.

"No Claim without Truth," the thunder said. "Show her."

"Very well." Brandon's deep voice echoed that thunder.

His left hand removed his sash with one quick tug,

sending his robe sliding to the ground. Hannah moaned softly as she finally saw his hard, stiff manhood, yearning for her with a fierce lust that matched her own desire.

His gaze locked with hers and he threw his arms wide. "Look upon my soul," he told her.

Light exploded out from him, threaded through with ribbons of purest midnight. They curled around his sleek, muscled body, rising, coiling, merging… and suddenly, a glorious black Dragon loomed above him, the molten pools of its eyes locked upon her face. With a roar that shook her, it spread its wings wide. Dominating, claiming the clearing.

And her.

"This is my soul." Brandon's voice grew softer, rough with desire and longing. "Can you bear its power?"

Could she? Hannah tilted her head back, staring at the Dragon above her. Power and desire radiated from its every curve – and now, having looked upon it, she could see those same demanding, hungry emotions reflected in Brandon's own face. His love was no weak, fickle thing. It demanded. Her body. Her heart. Everything. Now and forever. In return, he would hold nothing back. She knew this in her heart; the Dragon promised it. He would love her as no other man ever could. He would shield her, strengthen her, even lay down his life for her.

If she could surrender herself. Could give herself to him completely.

Hannah turned away from the Dragon, her heart singing. Because, truly, the choice wasn't hard. She had dreamed of a love like this. A man like this.

"I welcome you," she told him. "All of you. Your strength. Your fierceness. Even your rage. I want you."

The Dragon roared its approval as Brandon's sensuous lips curved into a smile. "Then claim each other!" it shouted. "Take what is yours."

Two steps and he stood before her, so close she could feel the heat radiating off him like a Dragon's breath. He raised the dagger and bowed his head. "Hannah Stiles, I, Brandon Lord of the First Flight, claim you as my Mate. Through the ages, let our souls and lives be bound." With that, he plunged the fang-like knife into the cup of water she held.

Both dagger and chalice vanished. Hannah blinked, unsure what to do.

No such doubt troubled Brandon. He brushed the robe from her shoulders, leaving her naked, vulnerable. Then his strong arms wrapped around her, pulling her tight against his hot, male body. She felt his manhood, his need, pressing against her as he raised her chin and kissed her. And she knew, in her soul, that he was all she would ever need. Her love. Her Mate. Her protector.

They sank to the ground, cushions of moss beneath them. Brandon leaned over her, his lips first brushing hers gently. Lingering on the fullness of her mouth. Hannah gasped with pleasure, and as her lips parted, his kisses grew stronger, more demanding.

His hands caressed the curves of her body. Exploring her, claiming her. Tracing her feminine softness, so different from the hard, taut power of his own male form. One hand stroked her thigh, her buttocks, and then glided to the swell of her breasts. A finger circled her firm nipple. Teasing, promising. She moaned with delight, her back arching, pressing against him.

Desire flooded him, answering her pleasure. His kisses grew harder, hungrier, demanding. He pulled her close, his embrace growing tight, almost painful, as his need blossomed.

But she trusted him. He was an Alpha, a master – of himself as well as others. As fierce as his desire burned, he did not lose himself. Though his kisses were still rough with longing, they grew gentler. Traveling down her neck, across her shoulders, then her breasts. Her soft moans grew louder, more desperate as his hand slid between her thighs, stroking her, sensing the aching need of her womanhood.

His hot, muscled body rolled above her. Their eyes met as he asked a silent question.

Her answer was to pull him down into a passion-filled kiss. Her legs wrapped around him. Surrendering herself to him.

At once, he drove into her. Hannah gasped as his hardness entered her, filled her. The pleasure of it scattered all thought and her fingers dug into his shoulders as irresistible need flooded through her.

He took her. Each hard, fierce stroke of his cock sent waves of pleasure screaming through her. She could feel his raging hunger, barely controlled, as he claimed her. Her pleasure swelled with each stroke, drawing helpless gasps. His harsh pants melded with them as his own arousal grew.

With a sharp moan, she came, her back arching as the crescendo peaked. His own cry joined hers as he exploded within her.

Gently, Brandon slipped to her side. For a time, they lay there, basking in the warmth of each other's bodies. In the echoes of the bliss they had shared.

Slowly, sadly, the pleasure dimmed. As it faded, it left behind one awkward question. Hannah rolled over and caressed his cheek. "I'm sorry. Did I scratch you? I…" She fell silent, unsure how to explain the wild, uncontrollable passion he'd drawn from her.

Brandon blinked in surprise – then threw his head back and laughed, a deep, booming howl of delight. Somewhere above them, the great Dragon of his soul echoed that mirth. "Oh, my love! I'm a Dragon. You could never harm me!"

She joined his laughter, burying her face in the warmth of his shoulder. He pulled her tight, kissed her head…

AND THEN SHE WOKE UP.

The room was empty. Dark. Sweat-soaked sheets surrounded her.

She was alone.

For one heart-breaking moment, she clung to the tatters of that wonderful dream. To the hope that those nocturnal pleasures were real, that she had found her soul's mate. Then reality came crashing down, crushing her joy.

It was a dream. It wasn't real. None of it.

Hannah curled herself into a ball and pressed a hand to her mouth as the first tears came.

CHAPTER 4

Morning broke; grey and rainy. Hannah showered and prepared herself for the day, but her heart wasn't in it. Did it matter how she looked? Her silly dreams of happiness officially died today. No, she corrected herself, they died last night after that awful awakening. As strange as the dream had been, with its dragon and 'claiming,' it seemed so real, so vivid. Strong enough to make her believe, for a moment, that she'd truly spent a night joined with Brandon in passion.

Reality didn't let her fool herself, however, even for a moment. As she stepped into the hallway, her host's angry voice filtered up from downstairs.

"Nonsense! That doesn't happen."

"It did." Amarie, the housekeeper. Cross and vexed, by the sound of it. "It does."

"Spare me your fairy tales," Brandon hissed. Hannah hesitated at the top of the stairs, unwilling to interrupt, yet strangely tempted to eavesdrop.

The elderly woman drew herself up as far as her small frame allowed. "Fairy tales are history for our kind. You ought to heed them." Then she turned on her heel and stomped off toward the kitchen. Brandon shook his head, muttering something, and stormed into the dining room.

Wonderful. She couldn't even hope for a pleasant farewell. Hannah waited a few moments, glad no one had seen her, then went to breakfast.

Which was, indeed, as uncomfortable as she'd feared. Brandon brooded silently. Every now and then, she glanced up to find him staring at her, his face dark with some emotion she couldn't decipher. Anger? Grief? Despair? Twice, he drew a deep breath and she dared to hope for a miracle. That he'd ask her to stay. That he'd offer to come with her. That something, anything, would keep them together a little longer.

Nothing did. Each time, he sighed and went back to poking his meal aimlessly. She couldn't blame his silence. No words came to her either. There was no way she could tell him how much that empty, false dream had meant to her. It wasn't as if he'd truly shared that flight of passion.

So, they stayed quiet. Through pancakes and eggs and a petite little quiche. When Amarie cleared away the last of the plates, however, he finally broke the stillness.

"You'll be leaving, then." A statement, not a question.

"Yes." There truly was no other choice.

"Now?"

Was that longing in his voice? Did he want her to say no, she was staying? 'Now and forever' as the dream had said. Yet, as much as she wanted a reason, any excuse to linger, what could she say?

Logic offered only one, disappointing answer. "Yes. It's a long drive. I should get going."

He nodded, his expression unreadable. Then another of those shuddering breaths shook his powerful body and he rose to his feet. "If you will excuse me, then, I have business that requires my attention."

"Of course." She rose too, her heart leaden, and turned toward the door. "Thank you," she added lamely. "For your generosity."

"Please." The warmth in that word drew her back. "Do not forget my offer. I will protect you and your family, no matter what. You have my word. If you need anything – *anything* – call me."

Anything? Surely, a conniving little voice in her mind whispered, she could invent some excuse to bring him up to the farm? She had to smile at her own greed.

Brandon smiled back, and the mood shifted to a gentle melancholy.

"I'll do that," she promised him. And she meant it.

Amarie trotted down the stairs carrying her small duffle bag in hand.

"I can get that." Hannah tried to take it, but the old woman neatly ducked around her, oddly spry for all her age. She wouldn't let go of the bag until they were at the door.

As Hannah stepped into the gloomy drizzle, the housekeeper patted her on the hand. "Don't worry, dear," she said. "Things will work out. When someone's being foolish, Fate runs them over and squashes them flat."

Hannah had *no* idea how that was supposed to be comforting. Brandon was right. His help really was a bit daft. But she smiled at Amarie and then left, disappearing into the cold, grey October rain.

CHAPTER 5

New York traffic was, as always, miserable. Six long, draining hours later, she finally made it to Beverly's Corner with a half hour to spare before the bank closed. The sooner she deposited Brandon's check, the sooner she could dispel the terrible cloud of debt that threatened her family. As she stood in line, she smiled, thinking of how shocked and delighted her parents would be to learn the reason for her trip to the city.

When she handed the check to the teller, the woman gasped. "Oh, Miss Stiles, that's a lot of money! Did you win the lottery?"

In a small town like Beverly, a question like that wasn't uncommon, or rude. There was no one here who didn't know her family and the tragedy that had struck them. "Believe it or not, we had an antique that was worth a fortune."

"An antique worth seventy-two *thousand* dollars?!?" Several heads turned at that outburst and Hannah felt her cheeks grow warm. Even Mr. Overton, the bank manager, peered at her through his thick glasses. She nodded, and the teller gave an incredulous laugh. "Oh, my word! I'm going to go through *my* attic this weekend! Maybe I'll get lucky too!"

Hannah's smile grew forced. Well, she knew what the town would gossip about this week. Not that it really mattered. She hadn't done anything wrong.

Though, as she turned to leave, Mr. Overton drifted to her side. "Miss Stiles? Could I have a word with you, in my office?"

"Sure, sir." Puzzled, she followed him into the small, sterile room. The little man closed the door carefully and sat down. To Hannah, he seemed weirdly nervous.

"Congratulations on your valuable discovery," he said. "That must be almost enough to pay off your family's debts."

"It *is* enough," she corrected him. "We won't need to sell the farm now."

He squirmed. "Oh? I, um, I had, uh, understood from Mrs. MacDunnah, over at Northland Realty, that your parents already had a buyer."

Okay, everyone gossiped, but this… this came close to straight-out bad manners! Primly, she shook her head. "There was an offer, but they haven't accepted it yet."

"It was a good offer, yes?" Tiny beads of sweat speckled his forehead. Why on earth was he so upset? "At least that's what I heard."

Her eyes narrowed. Who was sharing personal information like that? She'd let her parents know that Mrs. MacDunnah apparently talked *way* too much! "I wouldn't know." Not exactly true, but this was none of his business. "What I do know is that none of us want to lose our home. This farm is my parents' life. My dad grew up in it, and my grandpa! We're not selling it, no matter how much some developer offers."

"Yes, of course, of course." He fished a handkerchief out of his pocket and dabbed frantically at his forehead. "I'm sorry. Could you, um, excuse me for a minute? There's something I need to speak to you about but, uh, there's something… a thing… I need to do first. I'll be just a minute."

Her instincts growled that she should leave. Something here was *not* right. Still, she hushed those paranoid feelings. This was Mr. Overton, for heaven's sake! She'd known him since she brought her first piggy bank here when she was five. If he needed a minute, she could give it to him.

The minute passed. Then one minute turned to two, two to five. At the ten-minute mark, a secretary appeared to offer her coffee and the manager's apologies. The 'thing' (whatever it was) was almost done. Almost. He'd be here in (another) minute.

She had read every community service award on his desk – three times – and was just about to leave when the door behind her opened.

Energy swirled into the room, setting the hairs at the nape of her neck on end. A sense of something powerful, yet vaguely familiar, swept over her. Brandon! She startled to her feet, spinning around. How could he be here now?

The man who stood in the doorway wasn't her patron. There were vague similarities between the two men. They shared high cheekbones, a powerful physique, and the domi-nant air of men accustomed to being obeyed. And they both were stunningly handsome. That was all they shared, however.

The stranger was light to Brandon's shadow. Blonde hair, tinged with red highlights, flowed to the shoulders of his tailored suit. His 'friendly' smile never reached his brilliant green eyes, which studied her with cool disdain. As Hannah faced him, some ancient instinct woke within her. A tiny voice in the back of her mind that warned, 'This is a predator. Be very, very careful.' She had *no* idea where her crazy fancy – that Brandon had entered the room – had come from. The longer she watched the stranger, the more convinced she became that the two men were total opposites.

"Miss Stiles? Hi." The man held out a flawlessly manicured hand, which she shook gingerly. "Sorry about the wait."

As he offered his hand, the light glinted on the large cufflink that closed his sleeve. An elaborate golden knot, set against a blood-red stone. No, not a knot, Hannah realized. It was a Worm-like dragon, writhing, chewing off its own wings.

He was Mr. Overton's 'thing' that needed to be done? She pulled her hand back after that quick shake, puzzled and uneasy. Why had she thought he was Brandon? The two men weren't really all that much alike. "I'm sorry, Mr. Overton didn't tell me your name."

"Stephen LeMar. Please, sit." Though, she noticed, he didn't take a chair himself. He leaned against the doorframe, cutting off the room's only exit. The thought of him, looming over her in the small room, made her shiver. Like a dove watching a hawk circle overhead.

No, she wouldn't let him rattle her like that. Instead of taking a seat, she picked up her purse and slung it over her shoulder. "I don't really have time to talk. It's been a long day."

"I'll make this quick, then. I'm the president of C&L Enterprises. The investment company that made the offer on your family's farm." When she said nothing, he pressed on. "I understand that your family will – probably – reject our offer. So, I wanted to see if there was anything I could do to sweeten the deal. If there's a higher price you're looking for, name it."

"That's for my parents to decide. They're the ones that actually own the farm."

His smile broadened, the edges curling with a malign amusement. "But that's not exactly true, is it? Without you, they have no choice. You're the one who's bailing them out. You're the one who sold some silly antique for a small fortune."

How dare Mr. Overton share personal information like that! Hannah sent a silent profanity in the manager's direction.

Before she could complain, LeMar stepped closer. "And why should you do that?" His voice dropped to a deep murmur. "You're the one who figured out what that junk was worth. You're the one who did all the work. *You* deserve the rewards. Keep what's yours," he hissed.

He had a point... didn't he? A second later, she started in shock. No, he didn't. Not at all! How could she even think...?

Green eyes, cold as a lizard's scales, watched her. Stunned by her own sudden greed, Hannah managed to shake her head. "It belongs to my family. *I* belong to my family. I love them and..."

"And you want to end your days in this shithole of a town?" One of his thin, plucked eyebrows arched delicately. "Are you so lacking in ambition? In desire? Look at yourself! You're young. You're beautiful. Why should you rot away in this hick village, slaving for a family that doesn't deserve you?"

His words were stupid, foolish. And yet...

And yet, as she struggled to tear her gaze away from his awful, piercing eyes, a petulant greed swelled in her heart. Why *should* she give this to her parents? Even though she was twenty-three, they treated her like a child. Did they ever ask *her* how she could help? No!

LeMar slid nearer, close enough she felt the warmth of

his body against her shoulder. "That check was made out to you, wasn't it? It's yours. Take it. Take the money and leave." His voice grew rougher, angrier. "Leave these useless fools who seek to saddle you with *their* debts, *their* duties! Don't listen to them when they pretend to know your destiny. Take back your life, your wealth, your future. What do you want most in the world, Miss Stiles?"

Images swirled through her mind, like fragments of a dream. Silk clothes, bright and gauzy. A room full of elegant, jewel-covered dancers – and her at the heart of them, laughing.

"You can have these things." LeMar leaned close and whispered in her ear.

A tropical beach. Blue sky and pure white sand, stretching as far as the eye could see, and all of it for only her and Brandon.

Brandon.

His name, the thought of him, ripped through those poisonous temptations like a sword. The alluring images vanished, leaving Hannah feeling like she'd woken from a spell.

"With this much money, you can buy whatever your heart desires," Stephen promised her.

She almost laughed at him. Maybe some men could be bought. Brandon Lorde wasn't one of them. Nor could she put a price tag on her parents' love or her brother Danny's proud smile the first time he moved a leg after the accident. An achievement he owed, in great part, to her, and her tireless support.

Nothing was worth more than that.

She suddenly realized how close LeMar had inched as he spoke. How he leaned over her, touched her. Hannah's lip wrinkled in disgust and she quickly shied away. "Not interested," she snapped. "I need to go."

His head snapped back as if she'd slapped him. One second of confused disbelief and then anger flooded his elegant face.

No, not anger. Rage. Hannah gulped and fought the urge to flee.

He towered over her, teeth bared in a snarl, a barely controlled fury twisting his handsome features into a hideous, terrifying mask. "You *dare*? You deny me? You spit upon my offer? I will make you regret this bitterly, you…"

Run. She had to run, to escape. Faced with his vicious, inhuman rage, however, Hannah found herself frozen like a deer in headlights.

Tap tap! A light rap on the door shattered that tension. LeMar spun, fighting to control himself, as Mr. Overton's secretary opened the door and stepped in. Immediately, the small woman froze. His attempts to reign in his fury weren't completely successful.

He waved his hand at the papers she held. "Give those to me! *Now!*" The secretary did – then immediately bolted back out of the room.

Hannah was tempted to do the same – but she was not going to let this man bully her. As he scanned the papers, scowling, she gritted her teeth and marched toward the door.

"Stop!" he yelled. She froze. Silence fell beyond the door as all talk in the bank cut short.

He turned the papers toward her. Outraged, she recognized a copy of the check she'd just deposited.

"How do you know Brandon Lorde?" LeMar demanded. His rage had vanished, replaced by some dark emotion she couldn't quite name. It looked suspiciously like fear, however. That pleased Hannah, more than she wanted to admit.

"I sold him an antique."

"How did you meet him? Is he an old family friend?"

He actually edged away from her! Like she was... scary? Dangerous?

Hannah didn't stick around to find out. As the ominous stranger shifted out of the doorway, she breezed past him and strode through the shocked crowd listening in the bank.

Though she did call back over her shoulder: "That's none of your business!"

CHAPTER 6

*B*ack in the safety of her car, Hannah leaned against the steering wheel until the shivering stopped.

What was *wrong* with her back there? How could she think those awful things? Sure, life was rough right now, between the bills, the worry, and Danny's rehabilitation. But did she truly dream of abandoning her family? Of running away from everyone she loved? Was she that selfish, that greedy?

No. Her nerves settled, and she leaned back into the seat. She couldn't believe that of herself. She didn't think of herself as a fighter – but she wasn't a quitter either. Nothing meant more to her than the people she loved. She would never desert them.

Then why the temptation? And why were the scenes of earthly pleasures so vivid, so real? Nothing made sense anymore. It was like she'd been under some kind of spell. Hallucinating. Was she going crazy? She'd never had a dream like last night's, where Brandon claimed her as his soul mate.

34

Now this. Mad, cowardly urges to waste money on silly whims.

Movement in her rear-view mirror. She caught a glimpse of LeMar walking out of the bank, speaking on his cell phone. Hannah looked away, praying he wouldn't come over. When she glanced up, he was gone.

What now? Darkness had fallen while she waited in the bank. Back at home, Mom would be putting supper on the table. No doubt, they all worried about her and why she took such a mysterious trip yesterday. She smiled, imagining the look on their faces when they realized that she – their 'little girl' still at twenty-three – had saved the day. She'd found a gallant, rich stranger with enough money to redeem their home. Her smile faded a bit, growing sadder, melancholy. How could she explain Brandon to them? His strength. The raw, male power that radiated from him. They'd never understand.

Maybe that was just as well. The thought startled a stifled giggle from her. She certainly wasn't a child anymore, but she still didn't *want* to try to explain to her parents the raw, passionate desire this man made her feel. And something more than pure lust. A bond, a link, like she'd found the second half of her soul.

Perhaps, if they met him, they'd understand. If she could come up with an excuse to summon him to Upstate New York.

Wait. Her eyes brightened. She *did* have a question for Brandon! That nasty LeMar man seemed to know him. Maybe the two were acquaintances? It was worth asking. Although Hannah doubted the question would drag her mysterious protector all the way up here, she desperately wanted a reason – any excuse – to listen to his deep, rich voice again. To hear him say her name again.

Her breath grew shallow as she dialed the number.

Hannah forced herself to breathe, to calm down. She couldn't reveal her need for him. The embarrassment would kill her.

On the second ring, he answered. No greeting. No pleasantries. Just, "Brandon Lorde."

How like him, she thought with a fond smile. Strong. A brusqueness that was almost rude – if you didn't know the protective urge that lay beneath it. Though miles separated them, she closed her eyes and basked in the simple joy of hearing his voice.

"Hello? Is someone there?"

Oh, hell! She needed to say something! "Uh, hi!" Her thoughts scattered, and her cheeks burned as every coherent thought left her. "Hi, um, it's…"

"Hannah!" Delight dispelled the growl that had crept into his voice. Her heart hammered at the sound. He'd missed her! He felt the same longing as she did. Only a few hours apart, and it was already obvious in his happy tone.

That happiness lasted less than a second. "What's wrong?" he snapped. Already steeling himself to launch an attack on anything that threatened her.

"Well, nothing… exactly, but…"

'Not exactly' wasn't good enough. "Are you in danger?" She heard a loud rustle from his end of the line, as if he was already snatching up his coat and preparing to rush to her side. His fierce, unquestioning defense thrilled her. Filled her with an echo of the desire she'd felt when the dream united them.

"No, I'm fine. I'm safe. I…"

"What's wrong then? You're nervous."

"Well, it's just…" She hesitated, trying to come up with a way to make LeMar's ambush sound less crazy – but still scary. Right now, she wanted a protector in the worst way. Before she could organize her thoughts, however, Brandon decided he knew what enemy needed to be put down.

"Is the bank questioning the check? If they inconvenience you, I swear I will come up there and…"

Hannah gave an exasperated laugh. "Brandon, wait! Just… please, give me a second. I'll explain if you let me!"

That quieted him. Most men would apologize after running her over like that. However, she was beginning to realize that apologies weren't really Brandon Lorde's 'thing.' He simply hesitated, sighed, and said, "Please do."

"Thanks." Annoying as his fierceness could be at times, she loved it and the challenge of deciphering his veiled emotions. Her family always made their feelings plain, even when she was a girl. Brandon was different. His affection was so swift, so protective. What would it feel like to earn his full love?

Hannah shook her head to drive that thought off. She couldn't sit here, daydreaming, in the middle of a call. "The bank took the check," she assured him. "But something odd happened."

"Yes?" Brandon stuck to the letter of his promise: he didn't keep talking. Yet that one word was short and sharp, almost an order for her to hurry up and name the fool that dared to inconvenience her.

"Do you know a Stephen LeMar?"

He considered that question at length before answering. "No."

"That is so odd! He definitely recognized your name."

"Did he?" Brandon didn't sound surprised. "I guess it's not strange. I'm well known in, mmm, certain circles." Hannah waited, but he didn't explain what 'circles' those might be. "What did this LeMar character do?"

"He's the president of C&L Enterprises." Still no sign that any of this was familiar to Brandon. "He wants to buy our farm."

"Is he threatening you?" Her guardian's growl returned.

"Trying to pressure you into selling? I can have a vicious weasel of a lawyer there by tomorrow morning if this LeMar is bothering you."

"No. Well, he was, but he wasn't threatening." Not true in the least. But how could she explain that to Brandon? She couldn't say that LeMar seemed cloaked in power, a cold, bitter reflection of the strength she'd felt in him. He would think her mad. "He just offered us more money."

"I see."

Now she felt like a fool. She'd called him over nothing. Over a silly flight of nerves that even she couldn't explain.

Brandon wasn't writing her off so quickly, though. "Hannah, there are reasons why a Shif..." He coughed. "Why someone in my social circles might want to possess your land. Very badly. Many people in my circles could also offer you a great deal of money, if you were interested. Which I know you are not," he added quickly, as she started to protest.

Silence stretched. Just when she was about to apologize for wasting his time, he spoke again, voice soft. "This may sound like a very odd question. Did this Stephen LeMar remind you of anything? A person? An animal, even?"

A van pulled into the parking space behind her, its lights on bright. Hannah raised a hand to shield her eyes. "Actually, he did. He..." She thought of LeMar's rugged handsomeness, the threat of anger and power he radiated. "He kind of reminded me of you. A really nasty version of you," she added.

"There should not be anyone like me in Beverly." The growl was back, stronger than ever. Hannah, however, had absolutely no idea what he meant by that. "Was there anything about him that stood out? Some mark woven into his clothes? An unusual ring? Anything?"

How did he know that?

The van door opened. Its light stayed on bright and she prayed the careless driver would remember to dim them. "He had a strange cufflink. Red stone. It had an image of a weird dragon on it. Looked like it was tearing its own wings off."

"WHAT?"

Brandon's roar of shock and outrage blasted through the phone, startling her so badly she nearly dropped her cell on the floor.

"Why are you upset? What does that mean?"

"Hannah, listen to me." A fierce worry softened his words, though he ignored her questions. "You are in danger."

Her mouth went dry. Some part of her mind scoffed at the warning. Danger? In Beverly, New York? He couldn't be serious. Then she remembered LeMar's eyes, his incandescent fury when she'd refused his offer. No, she believed Brandon. She didn't understand his warning, but she didn't doubt it.

"Get your family and get out of town. I will take care of this. Stay at a motel. Do *not* return until..."

Her door yanked open.

Beside her stood a large man dressed in motorcycle leathers. A cruel, wolfish face leered at her from beneath thick, matted hair. "Time to go, girl," he said as he pressed a damp cloth to her face.

Hannah dropped her phone and grabbed his wrist, struggling to twist free. His hand never moved; it was like trying to bend an iron bar. Something sweet and rotten filled her lungs as she fought, clawing at him. Black clouds bubbled up at the edge of her vision, and the world around her faded out.

The last thing she heard as the darkness claimed her was Brandon's voice, frantically shouting her name.

CHAPTER 7

Smell returned first. Rotten food, stale sweat, and… wet fur? As her consciousness returned, dark, guttural growls came with it and an eerie scratching. Like the sound of a bear's claws on a tree.

Hannah opened her eyes, her head still pounding from the drugs they'd used on her.

She sat on the dirty floor of an old barn. Cold drafts seeped through the holes in its walls, bringing welcomed fresh air. The long-empty barn reeked of dogs and unwashed people. Half a dozen lanterns made more shadows than light. She lay slumped, arms twisted behind her back and hand-cuffed around one of the thick posts that held up its roof.

Six leather-clad brutes lurked by at the edges of the room. She recognized the one who'd grabbed her. Oddly, none of them seemed interested in the woman they'd kidnapped. Instead, they stared nervously at the floor ahead of her, where a familiar figure crouched, his back toward her.

Stephen LeMar. Somehow, that didn't surprise Hannah.

He crouched delicately on his heels to avoid soiling his suit in the dirt and rat droppings that littered the wooden floor. He was the source of the odd scratching. She couldn't see over his shoulder, but he dug at the floor with something she couldn't see. A knife, by the sound of it.

Gingerly, Hannah rose to her feet. The movement drew the bikers' attention for the briefest of moments, and then they returned to staring obsessively at LeMar. She flexed her arms as much as the cuffs allowed. Bumps, bruises, stiffness… but no major injuries. A tug confirmed that the cuffs were locked, and not toys.

It wasn't going to be easy to escape. What about rescue? They hadn't gagged her. LeMar didn't seem like the type to overlook something so obvious, however. If she *could* scream, it probably meant there was no point doing it. Several ancient farms lay scattered in the woods around Beverly. The nearest help might be miles away.

The scratching stopped. LeMar put his hand on his knee and considered his work.

No. Not a hand. A *claw*.

Hannah gasped in shock. What protruded from the sleeve of his immaculate suit wasn't a man's hand. It was a green-scaled claw, tipped with inch-long talons that glinted wickedly in the lamp light.

He turned. Seeing her shock, he smiled. Fangs filled his mouth. Curved daggers that had no place in any human being.

Drugs. It had to be the drugs they'd used on her. Hannah pinched her eyes shut as the room started to spin. When she opened them again, LeMar's hand was normal once more.

But the world wasn't.

Her kidnapper had carved… no, scratched an elaborate rune on the floor. Energy glittered in its crevices, a sickly yellow mist. LeMar kicked dirty straw over his work, then retrieved a handkerchief from his pocket and carefully wiped his shoes clean.

Worse, the bikers had shifted subtly in some mad, terrifying way. Their manes of hair seemed wilder, shaggier, like the coats of great animals. Yellow eyes reflected in the lamp light now, in a way no human eye ever did. And was it her imagination, or did their flickering shadows look like great wolves?

Drugs. Hannah swallowed and clung to that explanation like a life preserver. It had to be drugs.

"Right." LeMar tossed his soiled handkerchief aside. "I'll be back in the morning."

"Wait!" Hannah cried. Another voice yelled that word at the exact same moment: the biggest biker.

LeMar glanced between the two of them. "What?"

She spoke first. "What are you doing? Why did you kidnap me?"

"It's an experiment. You know what I am, right?"

"A jerk?" she suggested. "A treacherous, conniving Worm?"

To her surprise, he laughed with delight. "You have no idea how right you are. Do you?" His eyes narrowed suddenly. "Or are you less ignorant than I suppose?"

She had *no* idea how to answer that, so she just glared at him.

"You know you're Kindred, yes? No? No." He nodded. "As I suspected. You don't know what Brandon 'Lorde' is. You have no idea why he's giving you a fortune for some old thing. The only thought in your pea-brain is 'Oooh, how lovely! Look at all the monies!'" His voice grew thick with contempt. "I'd tear the truth out of you – if I thought you possessed it. Fortunately for you, you're an idiot. The information I could rip from your guts isn't worth the dry-cleaning bill I'd rack up for this suit."

Though her heart hammered, she fought to keep the fear from her face. She wouldn't give him the satisfaction of knowing how much he terrified her. "What kind of experiment involves tying a girl up in an old barn?"

"One that requires bait. The object you gave to Brandon. It was a gold coin, yes?" Although she said nothing, he continued as if she'd agreed. "I thought as much. I want to see if that coin was Blood Gold."

"I have no idea what that is."

"I'm sure," he said drily. "Trust me, if I thought you *did* know, I'd be disemboweling you right now. Dry-cleaning bill be damned."

LeMar smiled at her. Hannah didn't smile back.

"So, anyways," he clapped his hands and turned toward his minions, "if I'm right, Mr. 'Lorde' will show up here tonight."

Hope blazed in Hannah's heart. Would he really come to save her? Would he risk his life for a woman he'd only known a day?

Of course. He had given his word, sworn to protect her. Even after only a day in his presence, she knew it would tear his soul apart to break his word. He was a man of honor, and he would come for her.

"If I'm wrong – which I doubt – then you'll spend a mildly unpleasant night tied up here."

"And in the morning?" She didn't ask if he'd let her go. He enjoyed this vicious teasing.

LeMar bowed his head in mock sorrow. "Sadly, you just deposited enough money to cover your brother's debts. So, your family needs more bills." He turned to the largest biker, the one who'd asked him to wait. "I suggest a car accident."

"Like the one we did for the boy?"

They were the ones who'd run over her brother Danny?!? Shock and icy fury flooded through Hannah.

"No, no hit-and-runs. She knows too much. If you think you can pull off a coma, that would be great." As she stared at him in fear and outrage, LeMar shook his head. "Scratch that. Too risky. She could recover. Easier to make it fatal. I hear funerals are expensive too."

Satisfied with his plan, he strode for the door. Leaving Hannah too stunned to speak.

One of the bikers cleared his throat. "Wait."

LeMar paused. "What's *your* problem?" he growled.

"Where are you going?"

"Out. I don't explain myself to my servants."

True lupine growls rumbled up from all the leather-clad men. To her shock, their shadows twisted into the shapes of full wolves, crouched and furious. LeMar was not intimidated. He straightened, and his arrogant, domineering gaze swept over them. Under it, the bikers withered and ducked their heads.

Only their leader still dared to speak. "What are the six of us supposed to do if a Dragon shows up?"

She couldn't have heard that word. It was impossible. Though her throat went dry as she remembered the scoundrel's scaled 'hand.'

LeMar shrugged. "Try to survive? I'd suggest running away; it will probably improve your odds. Up to you. Not my problem."

Hair sprouted from the men's hands. Hannah grew dizzy as their faces lengthened and burst out with dark, shaggy fur. Angry snarls rumbled in broad chests. Yet none of the... Werewolves? Did she truly dare use that word?

She swallowed, hard. Yes, werewolves. Mad as it sounded, that's what they were. Uncontrollable shivers swept over her at the truth of that terrible, crazy thought.

And LeMar? What was so terrible that it cowed werewolves?

The pack leader was the only one who didn't completely submit. Hannah felt a grudging respect for the way he struggled to protect his pack. "Why aren't you staying with us? Together, we can take him."

LeMar sighed and began to speak in a tone adults used with particularly stupid children. "Because you're expendable and I'm not."

A chorus of snarls and snapping burst from the bikers. Their muscular forms shimmered, blurred. Clothes and leather faded, replaced by mangy brown fur. Before Hannah's astounded, terrified eyes, six wolves appeared where the men had stood a moment before. All of them bayed, howls of rage that resounded through the barn.

Stephen LeMar answered their anger with a fury of his own. Light burst around him as he threw his arms wide. Green scales flooded over him, and he suddenly grew, towering over both Hannah and his minions. His fingers twisted into lethal talons, his jaw lengthened, and a long, sinuous tail unwrapped from his body. In the blink of an eye, the handsome businessman had disappeared. Replaced by a raging, furious Dragon that threatened to shatter the beams that held the barn roof aloft.

No. Not a Dragon. Despite her terror, a calm voice spoke in the depths of Hannah's mind. Dragons had wings. LeMar had nothing. Just two masses of scar tissue at his shoulders where wings ought to be.

Shock and horror rose, almost overwhelming her. Nothing in her loving, ordinary life had ever prepared Hannah for this. Yet, now, in her darkest moment, she found a quiet strength. Faced with monsters out of legend, some part of her wanted to break. To give up and crawl, weeping, into the depths of her own mind. To hide from the danger and chaos.

She refused. She forced herself to look at the raging creatures howling for each other's blood. This wasn't drugs. This was real. If her safe, comfortable world fell apart, then so be it. She was strong enough to face reality, however terrifying it might be.

Because she wasn't alone. She had him.

Brandon.

What had they called him? A Dragon? Not a maimed Worm like LeMar, either, if a pack of werewolves feared to face him.

Brandon had sworn to protect her, and she trusted him. Her guardian would come for her. He would destroy the men who had dared to kidnap his charge. Though her life depended on it, she didn't doubt him for a moment.

"HOW DARE YOU?"

LeMar's scream boomed, shocking the pack into silence. "Dogs! Curs! You *dare* bare your fangs to your better? I should shred you where you stand!"

As quickly as it started, the confrontation ended. The wolves whined, twisting their muzzles away from the Worm. With a flicker, their lupine forms disappeared. Six men knelt on the ground, heads bent submissively to their Master.

The sight chilled Hannah. How terrible was this wingless Dragon, if he frightened men as strong and menacing as these Werewolves?

Hissing in fury, LeMar held his draconic form a moment longer. Then – silently accepting their surrender – he shifted back to his human form. One hand smoothed a crease out of the sleeve of his silk jacket. "Remember your place," he spat as he walked to the exit. In the doorway, he paused and glanced back at his whining, groveling followers. "And don't despair. I've left you a weapon. Use it."

A weapon? Hannah froze, wracking her brain. What was there in this decaying, empty barn that could possibly hurt a Dragon?

The door banged shut behind LeMar. The Werewolves

shuffled to their feet, angry and impotent. One caught her staring at him and anger blazed in his eyes.

Hannah dropped her gaze to the floor, as if he frightened her. Staring challenged dogs; it could drive a mean one into an attack. She bet Werewolves felt the same. Best to show some 'submission' of her own, if she hoped to survive the night.

That scattering of scuffed straw lay in front of her – and she gasped. The rune! That had to be LeMar's 'weapon'! It was the only thing out of place in this old barn. But how could a simple symbol be dangerous? Was it… magic? She hated to use that word; it felt insane to take magic seriously. Though was magic any more unbelievable than Werewolves? Something she now knew, beyond a shadow of a doubt, truly existed. If there were monsters in this world, then why not magic? What else could harm something as powerful as a Dragon?

She sank to the ground, tucking her feet under herself to gain a little cushion from the cold, hard floor. Then, holding her knowledge secret, she leaned back and waited.

Hours passed. The Werewolves paced, fearful and irritated. Sometimes, one would step too near a pack-mate and a furious spat broke out. Blows, bites, snarls, until the Alpha bullied them back into line. Hannah kept silent. No tears or words to draw their attention. Once, her leg cramped and she had to shift her weight. Even that tiny movement annoyed a wolf, who took two steps toward her before his Alpha cuffed him away.

In the end, the waiting ended without warning. Violently, and in a heartbeat.

With a bone-jarring crash, something large slammed into the ground just outside. The barn rocked from the impact, a cloud of dust raining down from its beams. Before a wolf could even howl, a great claw tore through the wooden wall and ripped the door away with one ferocious swipe.

There, in the ruin of the doorway, stood a Dragon. Scales as black as a starless night glinted in the lamplight. Ebony wings, sleek and powerful, arched from his back. This was a true *Dragon*, not some crippled Worm like LeMar.

Was it Brandon? Her guardian?

Yes. His eyes betrayed him. 'Eyes are the windows to the soul,' her grandmother had told her. And Brandon's blue orbs blazed in the Dragon's face. Set alight by some inner magical fire, but she would know – and trust – those eyes anywhere!

Werewolves screeched, howled, dropped to all four. The Dragon's tail lashed out, sending three of them sailing through the barn's thin walls. As they staggered to their feet, whimpering, one braver Werewolf charged the Dragon directly. Brandon's claws caught him as he closed, flinging the wolf into a beam. He bounced off and slammed into the floor, unmoving.

Seeing that, the three tail-whipped wolves traded glances – then turned and pelted into the darkness, howling in fear. Their last pack mate fled after them, yipping. The Dragon snarled with contempt but let him flee.

That left only the Alpha. He alone wasn't cowed, even by a Dragon. Still in his human form, he retreated to stand in front of Hannah.

Stepping carefully around that hidden rune.

The Dragon crouched, ready to spring. The Werewolf leaned forward, shifting his weight to his toes, preparing to dodge the attack.

As he did, Hannah picked both her feet off the ground and mule-kicked him with all her strength.

It almost wasn't enough. The pack leader rocked, barely

staggered. That tiny motion shifted his foot an inch, however. Far enough to touch the edge of the hidden rune.

A sharp, electric 'crack' rang out. Light blazed skyward, enveloping the wolf in a sickly green light. He jittered, dancing crazily like a man grabbing a live wire. Then he vanished, leaving only the smell of ozone, and burned fur behind him.

Hannah stared, shocked speechless by the destruction she'd caused. She'd... killed someone. A man. A wolf. A Werewolf. A...

A form hurtled toward her.

Brandon.

Her Brandon, not the terrifyingly glorious Dragon of his soul. Her fierce, human Protector.

He pulled her into an embrace. Strong, muscular, male arms wrapped about her, silently promising the nightmare was over. He was here. He would shield her, with his life if need be.

"Are you all right?" he asked, with a worry in his voice that made her heart sing. "I came as quickly as I could."

"I'm fine. I'm handcuffed here, though." She glanced about for a key – and prayed it hadn't been in the Alpha's pocket.

Brandon solved that problem. Reaching behind her (and pulling their bodies closer in the process...) he snapped the metal chain like a dry twig. Then, more gently, he drove his thumb through the metal of the cuffs and wrenched it open. Freeing her chafed wrists from their prisons.

Her jaw dropped. How could he tear apart handcuffs like that?!?

Well, he *was* a Dragon. She swallowed. It was going to take her some time to get used to that...

Later. She'd think about it some other time. Now, she simply leaned into his embrace. Cuddling against his shoulder. Feeling his warmth, the beat of his loyal, brave heart against her cheek.

Knowing her world would never be the same again.

Hannah didn't care.

This 'new' world had him in it. Her valiant, majestic Protector.

That, alone, made it a thousand times better than her old, comfortable life.

CHAPTER 8

As they stood, twined in each other's arms, Brandon felt his Dragon recede. The anger that had consumed him – fueled by fear for Hannah's life – slowly ebbed. He had her again. His woman. His soul mate. She was safe. And his.

Of course, the battle wasn't won. His enemies were merely scattered, not defeated. That battle could wait, however. What mattered was *her*. The sweet, feminine scent of her hair. The curves of her body, pressed tightly against him. Just like their forms had melded in his dreams.

"I'm sorry." Words which rarely crossed his lips came easier now. "It took me too long to fly here."

"You flew?" She peeked up at him, lips pinched with confusion. He longed, desperately, to press his own against them.

"Yes."

"There's no airport nearby. Did you… oh!"

Surprise, delightful and innocent, widened her eyes. Brandon nodded. "I'm a Dragon. I have wings."

He felt a twinge of worry at the confession. Could she

accept that? Would she shrink from him in horror? He prayed not. To see fear in her face – fear of *him* – would kill his soul.

He needn't have worried. His confession simply puzzled her more. "How can people not notice a Dragon flying over I-87?"

"People see what they want to see – and ignore things that don't make sense. Eh, that's not completely fair. Most people *can't* see us fully. They see... something they can't understand. So, they make up 'plausible' stories. I expect tomorrow's papers will be full of UFO sightings along the Hudson River," he confessed ruefully.

Hannah laughed. He watched the fear and tension drain from her face as she relaxed against him, knowing she was safe in his arms. Dragons didn't purr, but a deep, pleased rumble echoed from his chest. *This* was what his kind was made for. Protecting the weak and those they loved.

'Loved.' There was that word again. For the tenth time today, Brandon reminded himself that he couldn't love a woman the moment he saw her. What they 'shared' that night was nothing. Just a dream. No matter what Amarie believed, the Rite of Souls was a myth. Their joining – a union that had rocked him to the bottom of his soul – was an illusion. It hadn't really happened.

Lost in his own thoughts, he felt his love shift. He released her, savoring the gentle ache in his heart.

"Why can I see..." She waved her hand around the barn.

"Shifters. That's the word for our kinds. I suspect you see us because you're Kindred. That means one of your ancestors was a Shifter. You don't shift, but you can see those who do."

"And that?" Hannah grew somber as she pointed at the spot on the floor where the rune had been. Nothing remained except a thin, oily smoke. "What was it?"

"Hmm. Do you want me to give you the long, technical explanation? Or should I just say it's magic?"

"Let's stick with 'magic.' Today's been too weird already." She smiled, but it was a weak grin which vanished in a flash. "I killed him, didn't I? That Werewolf."

"Yes." Normally, he wouldn't honor those curs with the name 'Wolf.' They were ferals, strays driven from their own packs. They lost a true Wolf's honor, its wild independence, when they swore allegiance to a monster like LeMar. Best not to confuse Hannah with that detail, though. She was right. The events of the last twenty-four hours had destroyed everything she thought she knew about the world.

She rocked, silent, contemplating what she'd done. Gently, he brushed a stray lock of hair back from her cheek. "I hope you can live with that. The deed saved my life." Death and sacrifice came easily to him; he was a warrior. Could she face the cruel facts of war, he wondered? Or would guilt crush her spirit?

Hannah took a deep breath and gave a sharp nod. "That's all that matters."

Her words thrilled him. She might not be a Shifter like him, but a warrior's soul dwelled in her heart. Longing rose within him, and the urge to pull her close swelled again, almost too powerful to deny. His Dragon gazed down at them with approval. It assured him that Hannah Stiles, strong and pure, was a fitting soul mate for any Dragon. If the dream had been real...

...but it wasn't, he chided himself. Claiming didn't happen anymore. It had vanished when the Wellsprings faded from the world.

"What now?"

Again, her voice cut through his brooding. "Now, I'll get you and your family someplace safe. After that, I'll take care of this situation."

"No."

What did she mean by 'no'? He blinked, faintly affronted. He was Brandon Lorde. Alpha of the First Flight. Scion of Emrys, the Ur-Dragon, greatest of all Shifters! People did *not* refuse him lightly!

Except Hannah. "We can't just abandon the farm. There are animals that depend on us. They'll die if they're not cared for. And seriously? Do you really think I'll walk off and dump this all in your lap? No! I'm helping. We're doing this together."

Her protective instinct filled him with pride. How defiant she was! A tiny Dragon in her own right. But her loyalty was dangerous, and foolish. "These are enemies you can't fight."

"I know that." She met his gaze steadily, unmoved by the warning. "I saw LeMar. And you. I wouldn't stand a chance against either of you."

"Which is why I need to take you someplace safe."

"No."

Again with the denial! Before he could stop himself, he scowled at her, letting the edge of his Dragon's annoyance turn that look into a silent command.

One she completely ignored. "I don't plan to fight anybody. But I'm not leaving you alone. I can help you do whatever needs to be done."

"Hannah…" Why could she not just do as he ordered?

Because she truly was his soul mate, he realized. Her soul burned as brightly as his own.

That insight set his mind adrift again. To have a mate whose passion and strength matched his own. What would that be like? What joys, what love, could they find together?

"So, we're agreed?"

Brandon sighed. Dammit, he needed to focus. That foolish dream had filled his head with hopeless longing. Something he couldn't afford right now. If the Fangs of

Apophis were truly in Beverly, their lives were in danger. Any distraction could be lethal.

Arms folded across her chest, Hannah waited for his answer. "Yes… for now," he said.

"Good." She swallowed hard, still fighting to make sense of her new, insane world. "One last question. Well, two. Who is this LeMar guy, and why is he so anxious to get my family's farm?"

How could he sum up two hundred years of deceit and treachery? "I do not know this 'LeMar' personally. However, that emblem you described, the one on his cufflink, is the sign of the Fangs of Apophis. The Egyptians believed in a demonic serpent they called Apep. Apophis, in Greek. It was the devourer of souls. It sought to slay the sun, ending all life on Earth."

Her jaw dropped in shock and horror. "Is it real?"

"No!" He caught himself before a chuckle could escape. It wasn't really a foolish question. If creatures like him existed, then why not sun-eating snake gods? "Apophis is a myth. However, some very real monsters – fallen Dragons – take him as their symbol. The Fangs of Apophis, as they call themselves, dedicate themselves to greed and self-indulgence."

"Okay." Hannah frowned. "I still don't understand why these Fangs want my home. You don't go to a farm to indulge in anything except hard work."

"LeMar's motivation is still unclear to me," he admitted. "However, we know two facts that may shed light on it. First, the coin you brought me was Blood Gold. It's a token we Dragons give to a person who saves our lives. A sign of an unpaid debt that any honorable Dragon must repay. Second, your farm lies in *Beverwyck*, as the Dutch settlers called this part of the state. Three hundred years ago, there was a green Wellspring in *Beverwyck.*"

Seeing her confusion, he sighed. More complex things to explain quickly! "Wellsprings are… how can I say this? Places where the veil between the worlds grows thin. Portals that channel magic into this realm. Green wells, like *Beverwyck's,* were famous for their healing power. They're gone now. All the Wellsprings. They faded over a century ago."

Taking soul mates and the Rite of Claiming with them, no matter what dreams rattled him. Leaving Dragons with nothing to guard. Rotting, falling, because of the emptiness it left in their souls.

"Why would they vanish?"

"No one knows. The world has moved on. Grown colder, more scientific. Less magical."

She took this new information in stride and quickly put the puzzle together. "So, you think there's a Wellspring on our farm. Maybe one of my ancestors healed a Dragon at it and he gave us the coin."

"Exactly. I don't know why LeMar would care about that. As I said, the Wellsprings are in ruin, these days. However, it seems to be the only connection between Dragons and your land."

Hannah pursed her lips. A fetching look he allowed himself to enjoy for a moment. "Where's this Wellspring?"

"I don't know." He snorted. "I'm mature, but not *that* old! Does your family have any lore of a healing spring nearby?"

She shook her head, then her eyes brightened. "There's a bunch of ancient maps in the attic. Some of them go all the way back to the Dutch days. I'm pretty sure we've still got the first surveyor's map of the land. Maybe there's a clue in one of them?"

"An excellent idea!" He was warming to the idea of accepting her assistance. "Let us go to your home, then."

As they stepped through the ruined doorway, Hannah glanced around. "Wow. I can't see a hint of a road. Where are we?"

Brandon shrugged. "No idea."

"How did you find this barn if you didn't know where it was?"

"I didn't. I found *you*." He drew himself up to his full height and bowed his head to her. "Hannah Stiles, I have accepted the honor of repaying the Blood Debt owed to your kin. I ward you now. I will always know where you are. I will always know if you are in danger. And I will always protect you."

Enchanted by the odd, formal gesture, she swayed. Her full lips parted. Wonder and delight lit her face. Wonder, and delight, and…

Desire. He could see it, simmering in her eyes. A passion, a fire as fierce as his own.

Damn the foolish dream! Who cared if its promises of lifelong joy were hollow? She was still here with him, now. Even if the future was denied them, they could savor this one moment. He stepped toward her, ready to take the pleasure of her body and offer her his own in return. Her face tilted toward him, she spread her arms to welcome him…

And a draft, heavy with the scent of rat droppings, wafted out of the barn. Its foul stench instantly quenched their flames of passion.

"Ugh!" He turned away to hide his disappointment and frustration. "We need to get out of here."

"Yeah." She sounded as dispirited as him. "How, though? We don't know where we are."

"Hannah, do you trust me?"

"Of course!"

"Then I will fly us, if you permit. Once we're airborne, I'll be able to find your farm quickly."

Eyes shining, she clamped a hand over her mouth to hold in the giggles. "Of course, I'll 'permit'! How could I turn down a ride on a Dragon?"

Brandon smiled, but he didn't join her laughter. Hannah didn't realize what an act of faith this was. She was literally putting her life in his hands. Once they were aloft, only he and his strength stood between her and a long, fatal fall.

"How will you be able to find my home, though? Can you sense it the way you sense me?"

"No. I checked Google Maps after you left." Now her snickers did escape, and he felt mildly embarrassed. "I'm not completely medieval, you know."

"All right, my Oh-So-Modern Dragon, let's go home! Wait!"

He paused, holding his Dragon spirit at bay a moment longer.

"My parents must be Kindred, too, right? So, they'll see you?"

He nodded.

"When they see a Dragon, they'll think they're going mad…"

Brandon waited patiently, giving her time to reach her own decision.

Finally, she shrugged. "Let's do it anyways. They'll never believe me unless they see you. Besides," she added, as he allowed the power of his fiery soul to wash over him, "I'm not giving up my Dragon flight for anything!"

CHAPTER 9

Even hours later, in the boring, dusty safety of her attic, Hannah's heart soared with giddy delight.

She'd flown! *Flown!*

Claws – sharp and terrible enough to tear a truck apart – had closed gently around her. Brandon's precision was so perfect, so masterful. Not even a pinch to unnerve her. Then he had reared back, great wings unfurling above them. With a powerful leap, he threw the two of them into the air and carried them off with strong, unwavering beats.

Yes, she'd felt some fear in that first moment. Looking down at the houses so far below them. Knowing she could die if he made one mistake. But she trusted him. His strength. His complete and utter self-control. He would never allow her to come to any harm.

And so that brief moment passed, and she gave herself completely to the joys of Dragon flight. The feel of the wind rushing over her. The beat of his wings. Dipping and soaring as the gusts moved them.

Nothing had prepared her for that. Nothing in her life had been so wondrous, so joyful.

Well, except… that dream.

Hannah stole a glance at Brandon, bent over the old survey maps. Should she tell him about it? How much she longed for him? Needed him?

The memory of that passion woke a hunger inside her, which she struggled to ignore. What a ridiculous idea! She could never tell him she'd dreamed of him taking her in a mossy clearing. Claiming her body, her spirit, as his own.

Besides, he was a Dragon. A Shifter. What interest could he possibly have in a mere human like her? Even back when she thought he was 'just' a New York City millionaire, she hadn't dared to believe he might love her. Now? When she knew he was something far more powerful than any millionaire? No. It was hopeless. A Dragon could never love a simple farm girl like her.

Or… could he? Brandon called her 'Kindred.' That meant that some Shifter, at some time, loved one of her ancestors. If that unknown grandmother could be so lucky, why not her?

With a secret smile, she tucked that hope away in her heart. She'd dreamed once. She could dream, now, of even more.

A CLATTER RANG OUT FROM THE KITCHEN DOWNSTAIRS. MOM, cooking. Her parents took having a Dragon land in their yard about as well as anyone could take that sort of thing. They were stunned, terrified, numb with shock. In the end, however, they couldn't doubt the evidence of their own eyes. They, like her, were Kindred. Willful ignorance didn't shield them from the truth. Mom had eventually invited Brandon to stay for supper, a downright hospitable offer in Hannah's book. Dad even suggested he could eat one of the goats if he needed. Brandon assured him that no, pot roast would do just fine.

"What are you smiling at?"

She glanced up to find him studying her, not the maps. "Dad. And the goat."

"An… unusual offer." A faint smile tugged at the corners of his mouth. "Generous, if unnecessary."

"I was glad to hear that. I'm rather fond of our milk goats. If you had to… hey! Whiskey isn't a Dutch word, is it?"

"No. It's Gaelic."

"Then why is it written on this old Dutch map?"

Brandon stepped around the table and leaned over her shoulder. Her body stirred, came alive, painfully aware of his hot, masculine presence, pressing close. "It's, um, here. In the woods just north of here," she managed to say.

"'Whiskey' is the shortened form of 'water of life.'"

Exactly like the green Wellspring he'd described!

"We found it!" Hannah crowed with delight, then spun and threw her arms around his neck.

Immediately, she froze. Heavens, what was she doing?!? She barely knew the man! Lulled by the false memories of that glorious, passionate dream, she was treating him like her lover – not a kind benefactor.

She started to pull away, but he caught her arms and pulled her close again. Pressed tight against him, she felt his manhood awaken.

Clearly, she wasn't alone in her desire.

"I'm sorry, I should have…"

"Hush," he commanded. To make sure she obeyed this time, he kissed her. On her lips, her cheek, her neck. Exploring her, even as he had in the dream. One hand slid up under her shirt. A strong finger slipped inside her bra, circling her nipple, teasing, and her body came alive under the touch. Answering his powerful, masculine need with a yearning of her own. Energy blazed within him, the fiery longing of his Dragon soul. Hannah thought it could burn her up, so fierce was his desire.

Downstairs, the door bumped open. "Hannah?" her father yelled.

Both she and Brandon jumped. For a moment, his eyes burned at the affront of this interruption. His Dragon did not care to be denied. But Brandon was the master of his own soul, an Alpha. He would never allow his draconic fury to overwhelm him.

"Yes?" she called back, fighting desperately not to sound guilty. More from nerves than need, she brushed her dress straight.

"Danny's nurse called in sick. Could you lend me a hand with his bedding?"

"Yes. Um, of course."

"Thanks." He clomped off, leaving the door open.

A frustrated silence descended. Once more, the budding flames of romance died.

"I am so sorry," she whispered.

His broad, powerful hand caressed her cheek gently. "You have done nothing that requires an apology, my lady."

Hannah smiled at that old-fashioned word. And wished she believed him.

CHAPTER 10

The meal was stiff and strangely formal. Mom barely sat down at all. She buzzed about, serving people, popping in and out of the kitchen to check on a dessert that seemed to demand infinite attention. Hannah suspected she was hiding, trying to avoid their strange guest. She served Brandon awkwardly, bending forward to avoid touching the Dragon's arm.

Dad wasn't much better. Food sat, ignored, on his plate and he clutched his fork. Strangely tense, as if he feared he might have to leap to his family's defense at any moment. Whenever Brandon caught his eye, he realized how foolish he was being. He'd startle, look away, then shovel a great mound of food into his mouth and chew fiercely. But as soon as the Dragon's gaze turned elsewhere, he lost interest in the meal and returned to his obsessive vigil.

Still, Hannah didn't think it went too badly. Her parents had been through a lot today. Few things in this world were crazier than discovering that Dragons existed… and oh, by the way, your daughter brought one home for dinner. And poor Mom hadn't even seen Brandon Shift. How was she supposed to believe he was more than human? So, she forgave their clumsy attempts at courtesy and worked hard to keep talk flowing.

Danny was her wingman. Lying in bed, the boy had missed their arrival and thought their guest nothing more than a rich businessman. Unburdened by the knowledge of his draconic soul, Danny saw what mortals saw: a rich, handsome man who radiated power and authority. Being Kindred like her, he might have sensed something more. If so, he gave no sign of it.

Instead, he unleashed a torrent of questions. Did Brandon like football? Did he go to Giants' games, or was he a Jets fan? What was the best restaurant in NYC? How much did a real Rolex cost? What was the most expensive wine he'd ever drunk?

Her guest fielded these questions easily, with a cheerfulness that brought a fond smile to her face. She'd worried so much. He was a Dragon. A creature out of myth and legend. A millionaire who drank the finest wines and dined upon the most exquisite foods mankind could produce. What would he think of her, and her family? They must seem like hicks to someone as sophisticated as him. Dull country bumpkins full of boring, mindless chatter.

A burst of hearty, masculine laughter popped that bubble of worry. Danny had just finished telling some story. Hannah had missed it, caught up in those old fears. But, clearly, it delighted Brandon.

He didn't despise them. He fit in with her family, with an ease that warmed her heart. Okay, the suit was a bit much. It intimidated both of her parents. Brandon looked like... well, like a Dragon sitting amongst a flock of wood doves. Put him in a flannel shirt and jeans, however, and he could be one of them. And he was gracious. Some people stared at Danny's wheelchair and his scars. Not Brandon. He never blinked, not even when Mom had to feed her son because he still couldn't hold a fork steady.

Thanks to LeMar. A pinprick of fury, small but fierce, blazed inside her. He'd pay for that. Pay for all the pain he'd inflicted on her family. Maybe she couldn't beat him in a fight the way Brandon could. (For she was sure that, in a fair battle, the wingless Worm wouldn't stand a chance against her majestic Dragon.) But she could figure out what LeMar wanted and make *damned* sure he didn't get it!

Brandon glanced out the window at the dark sky. As he turned, Danny caught Hannah's eye and gave her a thumbs up. Like he thought his big sister had scored a really great boyfriend. She glared at him... then quickly wiped the look off her face as their guest returned his attention to the table. Danny smirked.

"Sunset comes early this time of year," he sighed. "I suggest we look for that spring in the morning."

She nodded, and he rose to his feet. "Mr. Stiles, is there a hotel nearby that you'd recommend?"

Of course, her mother wouldn't hear of that. No guest of hers had to stay at a motel! All that money wasted? No! Five minutes to change the sheets in the guest room was all it took and then Brandon agreed to spend the night.

The thought of him, so near, and yet, untouchable, stirred a hunger in Hannah. Something she'd never felt about another man or boy. Later, when she withdrew to her own room, she prayed fiercely that she'd have another dream. Even if she couldn't claim him in the real world, her night-time fantasies could soothe the ache, the yearning that filled her.

Sadly, it didn't. Her night passed in dreamless sleep. When the sun peered over the eastern hills, she awoke. Rested – and frustrated. Breakfast was a cheerful affair. Brandon devoured stacks of pancakes and raved about the maple syrup, made from a stand of trees on the farm. For the most part, Hannah just pushed her food around the plate. Mom barely noticed. She was too delighted by Brandon's greedy love for her cooking.

Afterward, the two of them headed into the woods, compass in hand. They hiked through thick orange leaves, stripped from the trees by an early storm.

"So, nothing about this 'Whiskey Springs' is familiar to you?" he asked.

She shook her head. "I hiked these woods a lot as a girl, but I never found a spring."

"It's probably dead then."

The thought of an enchanted spring delighted her. Why did he seem so cool, almost indifferent?

Not, not indifferent, she realized. Hopeless. Whatever these Wellsprings were, they'd obviously meant a lot to the Dragons. Dead Wellsprings were uncommon, but not unknown. Certainly, Brandon told her, a dead spring was nothing to excite LeMar's murderous greed. To her, the conclusion seemed obvious: The Wellspring wasn't dead. She suspected, however, that her love didn't dare hope for that much.

They quickly arrived at the site marked on the map. Nothing was there. No springs, not even long dead ones, appeared as they circled the nearby woods. Not even Brandon's dragon-sharp magical senses picked up any clues. "This was a waste of time," he grumbled.

"Hey, walking in the woods with you is never a waste of time!"

Her teasing couldn't shake the dark mood that had settled over him. "Let us return. There are other avenues I can investigate that may shed light on LeMar's motivations. Before I leave, though, we need to revisit the issue of protection. You and your family aren't safe here."

"Brandon." She put a hand on his arm to stop his restless pacing. "Let's spend another hour looking. It would be easy to miss a small pool in all these leaves."

He pulled away from her. "You don't *understand*. If a Wellspring were near, I would know it. Even a dead one."

"So, these things can't, well, hide? Or be hidden?"

"Yes. Of course, they can." He gave her a withering stare. "But such concealment requires magic. The Wellspring would need to be alive to do that."

And he wasn't willing to entertain that hope, no matter how tempting. Hannah didn't let his grim mood upset her. This must pain him far more than he would admit.

She was. "A live Wellspring would be valuable to LeMar, right?"

"Priceless."

"Which would explain his interest in this farm. So, let's take a little more time – just a half hour, all right? To see if maybe, just maybe, the 'impossible' has happened." He started to contradict her, and she interrupted. "Are you absolutely positive these Wellsprings are dead and not just dormant? Absolutely positive?"

He scowled, refusing to answer. She folded her arms across her chest and waited. "Fine," he snapped. "One half hour. Then we leave."

Good. Now where to restart their search? Hannah quieted her mind, hoping that her 'Kindred' senses (whatever they were) would pick up a hint of magic. No luck – and no surprise since Brandon had no idea where to go. He knew far more about magic than she did.

But not about forests…!

"Hang on!" She pointed up the slope ahead of them. "What's that?"

He followed the line of her finger. "I believe they're called 'trees.'"

She ignored his sarcasm. "Birches, to be exact."

"What, precisely, is the significance of birches?"

"Nothing – but *look* at them!" He peered closer... and suddenly, his eyes widened. Hannah grinned triumphantly. "It's almost November and they still have green leaves. Every other tree around us is dead. Well, dormant..."

"...but those birches are still alive," he whispered. Leaving an unspoken prayer that maybe the Wellspring itself survived.

Laughter bubbled up within her, a giddy delight. "Well, what are we waiting for?"

Hannah bounded ahead, buoyed by a giddy rapture. She'd done it! She found this Wellspring that meant so much to him. Brandon followed more slowly. He seemed dazed, confused. It took him a moment to catch up to her, and as he did, she gave his hand a squeeze. "Never stop hoping. Never!"

They pushed on together. Pride welled in her heart as they passed through the curtain of birch. She'd done this. *She* had given a Wellspring back to her Dragon! With that joy came the oddest feeling of déjà vu. She'd been here before. Somehow, she knew that. In a dream... in a past life... she couldn't say. Yet she had definitely walked this path before.

Slender birches parted to reveal a tiny clearing carpeted in moss. At its center lay a small depression in the ground.

Waterless. Empty.

Dead.

Hannah's spirits crashed to the ground. No! It couldn't be dead! Not after all this!

Who was the fool now, urging Brandon to keep hope? He was right all along. This was a waste of time.

She turned to confess that. As she did, her love stepped past her. Awe lit his face and he wobbled with the slow, unsteady steps of a man sleepwalking. At the edge of the dry spring, he stopped and turned slowly, bright with wonder. "We found it," he breathed. "*You* found it."

"But it's dead," Hannah protested. "Isn't it?"

"Dead? No!" He gave a short, shocked laugh. "Can't you feel it?"

"Mmmm… no?" Was there a lightness in the glade? An effervescence, like the air was filled with a million bubbles? Well… no. That feeling passed as quickly as it came, and Hannah wrote it off to her imagination.

Brandon, however, had no doubts. "Then look at the trees! The moss! They can feel what you can't. This is a Wellspring! The first one I've heard of in more than a century! Yes, it's weak. It's only beginning to awaken. But it's not dead! Not at all!"

Slowly, wishing she could sense that magic and share his joy fully, she walked to his side.

"You were right," he whispered, pulling her close. Strong arms twined around her, wrapping her in a powerful embrace. His lips pressed to hers…

…and the golden chalice vanished from her hands, his words ringing in her head: "Through the ages, let our souls and lives be bound."

Hannah jerked away, staring wildly about the clearing. In the daylight, dusted with dead leaves, it looked so different. But…

"I've been here before," she whispered.

"As a child?" he asked, confused by her shock.

"No. In a dream. A few nights ago."

"Odd. What… No!"

Now he spun too, his face a mask of surprise. "Oh, Amarie. You crazy old Witch-Hare." His voice faded, a mere shadow of its normal bass. "You were right."

"Amarie?" Hannah fought to focus. She'd lain here, cushioned by this thick moss, and opened her body, her soul, to his hungry exploration. She had pledged him her love here, and he had claimed her. No, she couldn't get lost in those memories now. She needed to think. To concentrate. To make sense out of all this. "Your housekeeper? What did she do?"

"She told me to believe in the Rite of Claiming."

That was no help. Each new bit of craziness just made her head pound. "Look, I'm sorry, I…"

"You dreamed of this place the night you stayed with me, didn't you?"

Her jaw dropped. "How did you know?"

Brandon stepped close and took her delicate hands in his own firm grip. "Because I dreamed it too. The chalice? The dagger?"

The delirious, maddening sex they'd shared? Words failed her, completely.

"I thought it was a dream. My longing for you, coloring my slumber. But it wasn't. It was magic, as my wise Hare told me."

Her pulse fluttered at her throat, driven by her pounding heart. "I don't understand."

"Once, back when the Wellsprings flowed, and the world was full of magic, my kind performed a ceremony called the Rite of Claiming. When a Dragon met his soul mate, he would know because the two of them shared a dream."

Images came back to her. *His silken sash sliding down over his lean, muscled flanks, revealing...*

"If she agreed – if she loved him in return..." He cupped her chin and tilted her face up toward him. "...then their souls were bound together. They claimed each other. Dragon and Mate. Destinies and lives forever entwined. Even death could not keep them apart."

Dizziness swept over her and she clung to him. Joy weakened her, turned her legs to water. Only Brandon, his strength, his solidness, kept her on her feet. "You mean…"

"It wasn't a dream. It was our fate. You're my soul mate. My love. The pleasures we tasted that night? We'll feast upon them, every night. That desire will become the foundation of our life together."

To have that… to have *him*. Every day. His passion. His strength.

His love.

"Then… you'll stay?" she whispered. "After this is done? I won't lose you when, when we…"

"I will never leave you. Never again." He bent his head and sealed that promise with a kiss.

Lips, warm and hungry, pressed against hers. The fire from her dreams roared back to life, filling her with a delicious ache. She wanted him. *Needed* him. Sensing her passion, his own desire rose to match her.

Quickly, he slipped his jacket off and tossed it on the leaf-strewn moss. A pale light glimmered in his sapphire eyes.

His Dragon, Hannah realized. She could see his soul in his very eyes. She remembered the great serpent's power and deadly strength. That memory didn't frighten her. She loved him – all of him, both man and beast. He would never harm her. She was his Mate. Brushing his hair back from those bright eyes, she kissed him. Letting her body tell him, in ways words never could, how much she hungered for him. All of him.

Her coat slid off to join his on the ground. Some corner of her mind noticed the fall air, cool upon her skin. Light, delicious, like the caress of a lake in early summer. Perhaps his Dragon nature warmed them; perhaps the Wellspring blessed their union and shielded them from the cold. Hannah neither knew nor cared. Eagerly, they shed their clothes, flinging aside the last barrier that kept them apart.

Then they stood before each other, naked. Man and woman, Dragon and Mate. Her gaze traveled his body. Rising up the powerful muscles of his calves and thighs. Lingering over his hard, thick manhood as it swelled with longing for her. Gliding across his taut chest, his strong arms. Arms she longed to feel wrapping around her, pulling her close.

He was the Greek god as her dream had promised. Not one detail of their nocturnal union was wrong, from his tightly curved buttocks to the hard eagerness of his cock. He was, in truth, everything she'd dreamed he'd be.

When her eyes rose to his handsome, strong-boned face, she realized he watched her too, drunk on the beauty of her body. His brilliant blue eyes burned with a fierce, draconic hunger that threatened to devour her. A yearning that demanded nothing less than a full surrender to pleasure. Yet, his touch – warm against her skin in the cool air – remained gentle, despite the relentless tide of passion that swept over him.

They kissed. Gently, at first, as he reined in his Dragon's lust and made sure he was the master of his desire. Then harder, hotter, with growing passion. Their hands explored each other, discovering their delicious opposition: hard muscles to soft curves, swelling breasts pressed close to lean, muscular chest.

She felt his manhood press against the gap between her legs. At its touch – eager, ready – she whimpered. Her legs grew weak and she sank towards the ground, prepared to let their union reach its climax.

Brandon caught her and pulled her into his embrace once more. "Not yet, my love," he whispered. "A Dragon can fly higher still."

He slid behind her, arms twined about her waist. One hand rose to gently brush her long hair aside, and with a sigh of delight she felt his touch on her neck. Kissing, tasting her. Caressing her with lips and tongue. One hand glided lower and cupped her breast. A thumb circled her nipple, teasing, making her breath grow ragged with longing.

The other hand… oh, the other stole lower still, to the damp hunger between her thighs. At that first touch she cried out with pleasure and pressed herself back against him. Felt his manhood, nestled against her buttocks, grow harder at the sound of her desire. Slowly Brandon stroked her, sending waves of pleasure flooding through her. Again, her legs grew weak. Yet he held her aloft, mouth and fingers driving her to heights of delight she'd never known. Another man would have lost himself in that lust. Not her Dragon. He was an Alpha, dominant, the Lord of his own body, his own desire.

With a gasp, Hannah broke away from his maddening caresses and turned to face him. As Brandon stroked her cheek, she curled her head onto his chest, savoring the faint, male musk of his body. She kissed the nipples of his chest and felt him stiffen, arch his back. Offering himself to her hungry mouth.

Lower she sank, devouring him. Tongue and lips teased their way down the flat, muscled lines of his stomach. He moaned, his fingers wrapping themselves in her long, blonde hair. Hearing his need, the cry of passion she drew from him, her own body burned. Lower still, till her breath whispered about his shaft. Hannah's hand rose to stroke his manhood. She kissed it, licked it hungrily, imagining it plunging into her.

Panting, Brandon sank to his knees beside her. He swept her into his embrace, lips joining in passion again, and lowered her onto the bed of coats. One hand brushed the dampness of her sex, testing her eagerness, winning a purr of delight from her lips.

That moan, that wordless, animal whimper of need, drove him wild. He mounted her, sliding between her moist thighs, and driving his cock deep within her. Again and again, claiming her – his Mate – with each eager thrust.

Hannah surrendered herself to that ecstasy, no longer even trying to hold back her moans of delight. She arched, joining his passion completely, wrapping her long legs around his hips. Each stroke of his thick manhood sent waves of pleasure washing over her. Mounting higher and higher until, with a primal scream of pleasure, he exploded within her. Their cries of ecstasy merged, ringing through the little glade.

Panting, Brandon collapsed beside her. Still caught in the echoes of that passion, she lay against him. The two lovers held each other, hearts pounding, as a scattering of autumn leaves drifted down around them.

CHAPTER 11

For a time, they lay there, entwined together, and the world seemed perfect. Hannah luxuriated in the lingering glow of their lovemaking. In the safety she felt in Brandon's arms. Yes, she now knew the world contained monsters like LeMar who would gladly kill or maim innocents. Yet it held heroes, too. Guardians and protectors, like the man she lay next to.

Her man. Her Mate.

Her Dragon.

Dream had become reality. She couldn't imagine a more perfect happiness than the one that filled her in this moment. He loved her. He claimed her. Nothing would ever come between them, she was sure.

A cold breeze stirred the leaves around them, and Hannah shivered. Brandon kissed her once more then rose to his feet and began dressing. "We should go."

She nodded. The warm, magical cocoon that had enveloped them seemed to have vanished. Quickly, she pulled her clothes on. When she was finished, she looked up and found him watching her with a fond smile.

"Oh, my love," he murmured. "There are so many things I want to show you. The cathedrals of Paris. Moscow in the snow. The Mediterranean at sunrise."

Names steeped in romance. Yet, as she listened to them, the first tendril of doubt unfurled in her mind. Yes, she would love to travel Europe. But who would care for Danny while she was gone? Who would lend a hand on the farm if she was off sunning herself on a yacht?

Brandon didn't notice the way she cooled. "I want to show *you* off, too," he promised. "At Cannes. At Montecarlo. At the Louvre."

With him at her side, perhaps she could dare those places – even enjoy them. They were alien to her though, and daunting.

Still, he didn't notice the way she bit her lip, eyes clouded. "Wait till you see the Met... Central Park in the snow... You're going to love New York City so much, my dear."

Shock, cold as a bucket of icy water, washed over her. He expected her to move?

Well, of course. What was the alternative? Was he going to put on a pair of jeans, roll up his sleeves, and lend a hand milking the cows? A Dragon. Milking cows. Seriously? What was she thinking?

But she knew the answer to that question. As her heart sank and tears welled up in her eyes, she knew it. She was thinking she loved him. That he truly was her soul mate. That she wanted to build her life around him.

"Hannah?" *Now* he noticed her discomfort. "What's wrong?"

"Brandon, I..." They were the hardest words she'd ever spoken, but she choked them out. "I don't think this is going to work."

"Of course, it is. My Dragon claimed you."

"I get a say in this too, you know!" she replied, with a flash of pique. That little bit of annoyance felt good. It saved her from dissolving in tears as her world fell apart.

"And you gave it – at the Rite of Claiming. You accepted. You claimed me in return."

"In a *dream*," she corrected.

He stared at her, baffled. "In the *Rite*."

"I wasn't thinking! I was just… just… dreaming!" she wailed.

Disappointment and confusion darkened his handsome face. "Do you not love me?"

Oh, how she wanted to deny that! To kiss his worries away. To swear that yes, she loved him, with all her heart and soul. That wouldn't help, however. "It's more complicated than that."

"Why?" She turned from him, unable to look on the pain she'd caused him, but he caught her arm. "Hannah, please. Talk to me. Tell me what 'complicates' our love. We can fix this. Together."

Anger had shielded her from her own grief. It faded away under the gentle balm of his kind words and now the tears came, pouring down her cheeks. "Brandon, it's my family."

"Do they not like me?"

"No! I mean, yes. Yes, they like you. But there's a chance that Danny will never be able to walk again, because of what LeMar did to him. My parents can't run the farm and give him the help he needs."

"That's a simple problem to solve!" he insisted, waving a dismissive hand. "I'll hire a nurse for him."

"We already have a nurse." Mrs. Grishom, a foul-tempered, lazy woman (who truly did *not* deserve the great references she came with).

He shrugged. "If her services do not suffice, I'll hire a second."

Irritation dried up her tears. Why did he think that all her problems would vanish if he threw enough money at them? Couldn't he understand that this was her baby brother? She didn't *want* Danny to depend on strangers. He deserved the care of someone who loved him.

"Then there's the farm. Danny planned on working it after he graduated. Now…"

Another casual wave. "Hired hands. As many as your father needs."

Hannah stared at him, cold with disbelief. Money again? Didn't he understand family? Obligations? Surely, a Dragon would at least understand honor? Flooding her family farm with strangers would change it, irrevocably.

"No." She wanted to say more but couldn't.

"Hannah…" He reached for her. She backed away.

"No. I don't want to discuss this now."

"But…"

"Let's go. We need to figure out what we're going to do next."

Though it tore her heart apart, she turned her back on him and began the cold walk home.

CHAPTER 12

*B*randon followed Hannah blindly through the woods. Branches whipped at his face; he didn't try to dodge them. Even in his human form, his skin was as tough as a Dragon's scales. He barely felt the blows – and cared about them even less.

His entire mind, his entire being, focused on his Dragon.

It raged. It roared. It *demanded* that he give in to it. That he let its wild power sweep over him and transform.

How could she do this? We are Mates! We claimed her! She cannot deny her destiny!

But she could. The human part of his soul knew that and, grieving, accepted it. Brandon didn't understand how things had gone so wrong. He'd never imagined that the world could swing from bliss to despair in the space of a kiss. Yet, it had.

No! Shift! Howl our rage to the skies until she sees how wrong she is!

A being of primal desire and energy, his Dragon could not understand how fragile humans were. How its power and anger could destroy a mortal mind. Dragons were not gentle creatures. Shifting now, when his Dragon raged so fiercely, would only terrify her. And he couldn't bear to see fear in her face. Fear of *him*.

No. He could not let go of his pain, his betrayal. He was an Alpha, the master of his Dragon soul. He would not lose himself.

"Are you okay?" Hannah's gentle voice broke the silence.

Brandon stared at her dumbly. How could she ask that? She had filled the cup of his soul with bliss. They had joined together, Dragon and Mate, and pledged their love with the wordless promises of their bodies. And then, at the moment when their union should have become eternal, she turned away from him. Rejected him, and his love. Then she asked if he was 'okay'?

She waited for his answer. "Yes," he said. "I'm fine."

"Okay." Clearly, she didn't believe him. Yet she still 'didn't want to talk about it.' So, she continued toward the farm.

A howl of primal pain welled up in him when she turned her back on him. Brandon staggered as his grip on his Dragon wavered. Scales, hard and black, flashed up his arms.

No! *He* was the master! He clenched his hands into fists. As his Dragon's energy poured over him, razor-sharp talons sprouted from his fingertips – and drove themselves into his own palms. As he'd planned. A Dragon was, after all, about the only thing that could harm a Dragon.

That shock of pain startled his Dragon, and in its moment of confusion, Brandon drew its power back into himself. Locking it safely on the Other Side. Claws vanished. Scales faded to human skin. Once again, he controlled himself.

Sensing that burst of power, Hannah glanced back, her face creased with worry.

Brandon gave her a smile. A stiff, fake smile – yet it seemed to reassure her.

Denied an outlet into the mortal world, his Dragon

keened with grief and loss. Though the danger of losing control was real, he couldn't be angry with it. He understood, in a way Hannah didn't, how much she'd hurt them.

Dragons guarded. The urge to protect filled them, in every scale, every drop of blood. Since the age of myth, they protected. Sacred places, like the Wellsprings. Sacred people, like their Mates. When the Wellsprings faded, they took the Dragons' hearts with them. Robbed of their purpose, their love, some went mad and chewed their wings off. Like LeMar.

Brandon knew the urges that had destroyed his enemy. The cold, dull greyness that life became when it held no hope of love, of purpose. He had tasted the seductive allure of greed, the urge to submerge himself in the empty, petty pleasures that wealth offered. So many Dragons fell to that siren song of despair and greed.

Today, he had dared to dream that his longing was over. That Hannah could fill the hollow inside him, the emptiness that threatened to devour his soul and turn him into a depraved, evil reflection of himself. As LeMar had done. She, and the crippled Wellspring, would save him from that. By devoting himself to her, to protecting her family and home, he could finally become what he was meant to be.

A true Dragon, whole and complete. A Guardian.

And now that dream lay shattered. Destroyed by one simple word: "No."

Despair washed over him and with it a lethal urge to shift and tear his own wings to shreds. Brandon closed his eyes until that mad desire passed and he was himself again.

I will not let you do this, he told his Dragon firmly. *Remember this: if one word destroyed our dreams, then another word can bring them back to life.*

Yes.

He would not rail at Hannah, would not let his Dragon

lash out in its pain and harm her. When she was ready, she would talk. He would listen to her. In time, he would understand why she denied him. And then, he would change her mind.

He knew he could. Her body had whispered that message to him, as she moaned in the ecstasy of their union. She had claimed him as surely as his Dragon had claimed her. Whatever obstacles her mind might imagine, her heart knew they were soul mates. Destined to be together. When he understood her fears, he promised himself he would solve them. More gently, less brusquely this time. For now, he simply needed to give her time. To wait until she was ready to face this with him.

Furious annoyance radiated from his Dragon. Dragons were not patient by nature.

But he was. And he would not be dominated – not even by his own soul.

A BLUE SEDAN WAS PARKED BESIDE THE STILES' PORCH. Brandon spotted it the moment they stepped from the woods, but Hannah reassured him. "That's Mrs. Grishom's car. She's Danny's nurse. She was feeling sick yesterday and didn't come by. I guess she's better." Her nose wrinkled. "Or maybe she just didn't feel like working yesterday. She's not very reliable. We really ought to find a replacement."

"I will see to that," he promised her. "Your brother deserves the best care." Having determined that the car and its driver were not threats, he turned to other matters.

Delicate ones. Ones he needed to broach diplomatically. "We need to get you and your family to safety. Only for a short time." He raised a hand to interrupt before she could protest. "I know how much this farm means to your family.

Remember, though, LeMar threatened to kill you. We can't give him an opportunity to do that."

She paused on the porch steps, sick with worry. "For how long? Will we ever be safe again?"

"Of course!" Without thinking, he stroked her cheek. At the contact, he hesitated. They hadn't touched since their moment of passion. Would she ever want him to caress her again? Then she smiled, and relief washed over him. "I will protect you, Hannah, and this place. You are both very dear to me."

He yearned to say more. To tell her of the emptiness her love filled in his soul.

Restraint, he warned himself. Give her time. We've touched. We've taken the first baby step toward reunion. Let it be.

"You're dear to me, too," she whispered, her eyes growing damp. Another tiny step. Even his Dragon grew quiet, sensing there might be some value to patience after all.

"Good. So here is my thought." Normally, he would simply tell her what they were doing. He was an Alpha. He ordered. Subjecting his plans for another's approval was an alien concept. Judging from his Mate's own strength of mind, however, it was something he needed to get used to.

"Let's get your family to my home in New York. Amarie is a doting nurse. I am certain she would love to care for your brother. I will stay here and…"

"Not alone!" she cried. "You can't! It's not safe!"

Silly as it was, her concern delighted him. She cared. No matter how much she swore they'd never be together, her own heart betrayed her. She loved him as much as he loved her. "Dearest, no Worm could threaten a Dragon. The mere chance of encountering me terrified him. You saw that."

Hannah scowled, not reassured. "I also saw the magical trap he left for you. Which vaporized a Werewolf Shifter."

Okay, she had a point. Knowing he could never defeat a Dragon in a fair fight, LeMar would, no doubt, resort to trickery and spells. Brandon, however, was certain he could manage that. "Honestly, I doubt he'll bother. Now that I know about the Wellspring, I expect our enemy will flee town quickly. Probably today."

"But the Wellspring is alive!"

"Barely. It's not strong enough to heal, as it should."

"It's still priceless, isn't it?" she protested.

"Yes, of course," he explained, with pained patience. "It's also now guarded by a Dragon. Which he cannot defeat."

"By himself. If he gets reinforcements, though..."

Sweet scales and teeth, could she not let it go? This 'democracy' nonsense vexed him and his Dragon both. Why couldn't she just let him give the orders, as he did with Amarie?

Because, he realized, she might be human, but her soul was as fierce as his own. Could he do what he demanded of her? Could he let her face an enemy without him to protect her?

No. Never. While Hannah might not be a Dragon, she understood the burning love that lay at a serpent's heart. He needed to be patient, as unnatural as it was.

"I will summon reinforcements of my own," he promised. "There is a Shifter family in Ohio that owes me a favor. They're not warriors, however, they could be here by this evening and care for your farm. I'll also summon my Flight. Other Dragons. Trust me," he smiled. "Not even the Fangs of Apophis dare to face a full Flight of Dragons."

She wasn't happy with his plan – but she couldn't find a flaw in it.

"Remember, this is only for a short time. Once my Flight and I have secured this area, you can return. I doubt you'll be away more than a week."

"And then?"

"Then we'll discuss… other things." What that might be, he left unsaid. Yet, she knew. They *both* knew that, no matter what words had passed between them, they couldn't simply walk away from each other. They were Mates, their souls bound by destiny. If life threw obstacles in their path, they would find another road forward.

Hannah sighed and gave him a rueful smile. "Okay. Sounds like a plan."

Ha! She agreed with his, um, 'orders.' "It's settled then. Shall we go in and convince your parents?"

The door behind his love opened. Standing on the step below her, he couldn't see the person who stepped out.

And he didn't need to. A waft of foulness – garbage and uncleaned fur – touched his Dragon's fine senses.

"Mrs. Grishom!" Hannah said. "How nice to…"

"Rat!" Brandon thundered. With one swift bound, he mounted the stairs, placing his body between his Mate and this sudden threat.

The woman before him quailed with a squeal of fear that betrayed her Rat Shifter nature. Contempt filled him. Him or his Dragon's, he couldn't say. Neither of them held much respect for this treacherous kind. One of LeMar's stooges, no doubt. He called his Dragon to him, letting its power roll across his skin. As scales flashed across his lean body, he glared at Mrs. Grishom, fully expecting her to flee.

In that moment, he forgot one of the great truths about rats: that, when cornered, they'd fight.

A jacket lay folded across her arm. From under it, the woman drew an obsidian dagger. She flailed wildly; Brandon swatted the blow away, lest it harm Hannah. To his shock, the black blade sliced through the plated skin of his hand. The wound was nothing – a scratch that barely bled. Yet the knife's track burned like acid.

With a shriek, Grishom collapsed into an oily rodent the size of a large dog. The knife clattered to the porch as she bolted for the woods at a dead run.

He spun, prepared to pounce on her and end her miserable life. At his movement, the world twirled madly, sending him crashing into the porch railing.

"Brandon!" Hannah darted to his side as his legs gave way. "What's wrong?"

"P-p-poison! You need to…"

That was all he managed to choke out before the darkness took him.

CHAPTER 13

"*B*randon!"

Hannah dropped to her knees beside him, cradling his head.

The front door banged open again. Drawn by the shouts and roars, her father barreled out, cradling a shotgun in his arms.

"It's Mrs. Grishom! She's a monster!" Hannah pointed in the direction the Shifter had run but there was no sign of the bloated Rat. Her treacherous blade might be able to hurt Brandon, but the coward still wouldn't risk facing his wrath.

Her poor baffled father knelt beside her. "What the hell happened?"

"Poison. Danny's nurse must be one of the Shifters who are trying to steal our farm." Heart hammering, her fingers went to his throat and found a pulse. Fast, erratic – but he was alive!

For now. Until the venom did its work.

Fear shook her then. A soul-killing dread that dwarfed any terror she'd ever known. What if he died? What if she lost him?

A half hour before, she'd told him they had no life together. Now, facing his loss, she realized how foolish she'd been. There was no future without him – none she wanted to be a part of. She could no more survive his loss than the loss of half her soul.

With a wail, she slammed her fist into the porch floor. Like an icicle, the pain sliced through her panic, leaving her clear headed.

"I'll call 9-11," her father said.

"No. He's a Dragon, Dad. They can't do anything." But who could? Where could she find help against a magical Dragon-slaying poison? Those Ohio Shifters? Brandon's Flight? Or…

…within herself?

"Dad, help me!" She slung one of his arms over her shoulder and tried to tug him to his feet. "We need to get him to that spring we found."

The Wellspring. Ohio and his missing Flight were too far away. Only the dormant healing well was close enough to save him.

If she could find a way to summon its magic back into this world.

"Honey, here. Let me." Dad set the gun down and hefted Brandon onto his shoulders in a fireman's carry. He rose to his feet, grunting in surprise at the man's weight. "Lead on."

Hannah snapped up the shotgun and ran for the woods.

In her heart, it took *hours* to reach the Wellspring. She wanted to scream at her father to hurry, that Brandon's life and hers depended on speed. One look at Dad's red, sweating face told her, though, that he was moving as fast as he could. A dozen times, panic threatened to drag her under. They were too slow. He was dead. It was all her fault. Each time that mind-numbing fear reared its head, she forced it back down. She had to stay in control. Brandon depended on her.

After an eternity, she saw a flash of birch leaves ahead. "We're there, Dad! We're there!"

They burst into the clearing. Her father staggered to the edge of the dry pool and collapsed, dumping himself and his burden to the ground. "What... what *is* this place?" he gasped.

"It's a Wellspring. It's magic." Hannah scanned the glade frantically, searching for any change. A whisper of arcane energy... a voice, promising help... healing waters bubbling up from the cold earth...

Something?

Anything?

Despite her unspoken plea, the glade remained unchanging. Strangely green for an autumn day – but drained of all power.

"Please..." Now she did speak, begging the Wellspring to aid her. "Heal him."

Nothing happened. The fall breeze swept her prayers away, unanswered.

"Honey?" Her father's voice was rough. "Sweetheart... I can't feel a pulse anymore."

No! She covered her face with her hands, as if her sorrow could be held back by flesh alone. She couldn't lose him! There *had* to be a way to bring the Wellspring back to life!

Think! She rocked, struggling to recall what little she knew about this place. It was a Wellspring, a pool of magical healing. What else had Brandon said?

'...a place where the Veil between the worlds grows thin...'

Thin.

With a flash of hope, Hannah raised her arm and slammed her palm down on the spring's rocky bottom.

She expected pain, stones tearing into her soft flesh. Instead, her hand collided with a soft cushion that gave way beneath her blow. Her hand sank into the ground… then her wrist… then her elbow.

It worked! Her elation died immediately when she glanced at Brandon who still lay, motionless, beside Dad. Though her arm sank deep into the earth, the ground around it remained barren.

Dead. Like her love would be soon, if she couldn't rouse the Wellspring.

Leaning forward, she fought to press her arm deeper, but it wouldn't budge. The Veil between the worlds, it seemed, only bent so much.

Now what? How could she be so close and still fail?

With a frustrated cry, Hannah threw her full weight on her arm. She would tear a tunnel between the Worlds with her bare hands if that was what it took to save her Mate!

Nothing. No movement. It seemed the Veil was stronger than she was.

Despair rose, threatening to overwhelm her. At its soul-killing touch, she wailed – and something on the Other Side answered her scream. A faint warmth brushed against her finger-tips. When she snatched at it, it vanished.

She tensed, ready to throw herself at the Wellspring again…

And then she saw her error.

Brute force would never conquer a Dragon. So why would a Wellspring, the sanctum that held the hearts of all Dragons, be beaten by it?

Love conquered Dragons. Love of Mate and home. Love ruled them, made them whole.

Love was the key to the Wellspring.

She relaxed, letting her arm rest in the well's hidden depths, and filled her mind with *him*. Brandon. Her love. Her Dragon. The masculine perfection of his sculpted body. The power with which he took her, claimed her, and brought her to the heights of pleasure. The fierceness of his great scaled form, terrifying to enemies, a haven to innocents.

She loved him, with all her heart and soul. Dragon and Man, she loved all of him. She called to the Wellspring – with love, not fear – to join her love.

And the Wellspring answered. Energy blazed on the Other Side, sending bright lances of light shooting into the air. Power exploded around her hand, like a thousand suns bursting into life. It roared up her arm, electric pulses racing along her nerves, up her body. (As it washed across her stomach, something deep inside her stirred. The tiniest seed of a someone stretching in joy as magic filled her womb. Tears of happiness filled her eyes as she understood the promise their love-making had left behind.)

With a hiss like a tiny drake, water rushed up around her elbow. It poured across the dusty stones. Dry moss greened, thickened, as flickers of light and magic rose into the air, banishing all darkness from the clearing. Hannah withdrew her arm and rocked back on her heels in shock. The pool of her dream lay before her.

Magic had returned to the world.

"Okay, I didn't see that one coming," said a snide voice behind her.

LeMar! Hannah whirled, jumping to her feet.

The worm stood by the birch curtain, a gloating smile plastered across his coldly handsome face. "I mean, I knew you were Kindred," he continued, ambling toward her. "I guess your great-grammykins was a Witch-Hare. Congratulations, girl. I planned to kill you, but you know what? I think you might be useful. Guess I'll keep you instead."

"Keep *this!*" Hannah snarled. She scooped the shotgun off the ground and let the worm have both barrels.

The force of the shot rocked him backward. The front of

his bespoke jacket exploded – to reveal scales. A hard, impenetrable shell her weapon hadn't even scratched.

LeMar's eyes lit with outrage. "You impudent vermin! That was my favorite suit."

Talons ripped through the tips of his fingers and a sickly yellow light blazed in his eyes as he summoned his Worm.

Beside her, her dad rose and stepped between them, his big, strong hands balled into fists. "You stay away from my daughter!"

"Dad, no!" she cried. He'd never seen a Dragon fight! He didn't know he stood no chance against one, not even a maimed, fallen Worm like LeMar.

"Two for one, darling," the Worm snarled as the last traces of his human form faded away. "You get to watch your Mate *and* your father die today."

"No."

Harsh, ragged with pain, that denial still boomed through the clearing. A shadow fell over her. She spun…

Brandon!

Above her loomed a magnificent black Dragon. He reared, wings sweeping out to form a protective shield over her and her father. The Dragon's burning sapphire eyes were fixed on the cringing Worm. "No one dies today," he roared. "Except *you.*"

Close to her Dragon, Hannah could see the faintest tremor in his legs, the way he shifted to keep his balance. That poison had ravaged his body, weakened him. Although the Wellspring had saved his life, he was still injured.

Her heart froze. No wound, not even a mortal one, would stop a Dragon from defending his Mate. Injured as he was, though, could a Worm defeat him?

If he had been a Dragon – or a man – LeMar might have stood a chance. But he was a coward, through and through. The sight of a true Dragon towering over him, filled with righteous, protective rage, broke his spirit. Screeching in terror, he whirled and fled, slithering off through the trees.

Brandon threw himself into the air… or tried to. At the last instant, however, his injured leg gave way. One great wing clipped a birch tree, shearing it in half. The Dragon rose a few feet off the ground, tilted, then righted himself with slow, heavy wing beats. The sight horrified her. Yesterday, when he carried her home, he had been the Lord of the Air. One powerful leap had sent both of them soaring to the heavens. Now, ravaged by poison, he fought to even stay aloft.

"Wait!" Hannah waved at him, trying to draw him back. He couldn't do this! Her feeble healing hadn't given him enough strength!

If he heard her plea, he gave no sign. Brandon rose unsteadily above the trees and pursued his fleeing enemy.

The sound of his wings faded, leaving Hannah to stare helplessly at the sky above her.

A soft groan, almost a whimper, drew her attention back to the grove.

Dad stood beside the Wellspring, rocking back and forth. Shivers shook his heavy body and he stared at the woods, slack-jawed with shock.

"Dad? Are you okay?" She stepped to his side and put a hand on his elbow.

"Those claws! God, those claws… and scales… and…"

She slipped her arms around her father and hugged him. Seeing a Dragon carry your daughter home was bad enough. A shock that could drive a lesser man mad. But to face one in full rage… to feel its roar shake your body… to be rocked by the buffets of its wings… That was too much to ask. She trusted Brandon. In her heart, she knew he would never harm her.

Her father had no such faith. Hannah prayed that the

sight of Brandon's true power would make Dad fear her Mate.

No, not her 'Mate'. Hannah winced at how easily that word popped into her mind. How natural it felt. She had to stop thinking of Brandon that way, or she'd never find the strength to stay true to her family.

Still, Mate or no, Brandon was a loyal guardian. An honorable man who didn't deserve to be feared by those he protected with his life. "Dad, come on." She gave him a gentle shake, hoping to nudge him away from the edge of his panic. "Let's go home."

"But he… they…" Dad's eyes scanned the sky for any sign of the two Shifters.

"*Brandon*," she stressed his name, "will take care of this."

At least she prayed he would.

"There's nothing we can do. C'mon. It's cold. Let's go back to Danny and Mom. I'm sure Brandon will meet us back there."

On leaden feet, her father followed her. At first, he stumbled, blind to the roots and rocks underfoot. But as they left the magic Wellspring and entered the woods – woods her father had played in as a boy – he grew calmer. To Hannah's relief, the comfort of familiar lands took the edge off his fear. Every step took them, literally and spiritually, a little further from the shock of warring Dragons. By the time they reached the edge of the farm, Dad had regained control of himself. Though he was still pale and damp with sweat, he stayed steady on his feet.

And he didn't even flinch when they rounded the corner of the porch to find Brandon, back in human form, sitting on the step beside Mrs. Grishom's abandoned jacket.

"Brandon!" He was alive! Safe! Hannah's heart leaped as she dashed to his side.

Her Dragon drew back from her. For one moment, his

eyes, dark with grief, met hers. Then he hung his head, unable to meet her gaze.

He was... ashamed? Her delighted charge slowed, stopped. "Are you alright? Is he... is LeMar dead?"

"No. I could not catch him. I..." With a grimace, he spat the next words out. "I let him escape."

Oh, was that all this was about? Once more relief washed over her, leaving her so giddy that she almost laughed. "Don't worry about it! You're safe. That's all that matters."

"It is *not* all that matters!" he snapped.

She sank to the stairs beside him and squeezed his hand. "Yes, it is, because as long as you're alive there's always tomorrow. We'll get him next time."

Brandon wouldn't be comforted. He pulled his hand away, still unwilling to face her. "There won't be a next time. LeMar will never confront me. He'll run as far as he can, and I'll never find him."

"Okay. So, you drove him off. That's still good, right?" Honestly, why was he so fixated on killing the Worm? Maybe it was a Dragon thing?

"You don't understand."

"What I understand..." She picked his hand up again and held it firmly this time. "...is that you're alive and we saved your Wellspring. Aren't those good reasons to celebrate?"

Now he did look at her, his face tight with misery. "Oh, we've saved the Wellspring alright. But I have failed, utterly, to repay the Blood Debt owed to your family."

"Only for today..."

"No. Forever. Hannah, we saved the Wellspring. But my failure just destroyed your farm."

CHAPTER 14

*S*itting around the kitchen table, it was hard for Hannah to take Brandon seriously. Everything *seemed* normal. Danny off in his room playing video games. Mom and Dad beside her, sipping coffee. It could have been a morning from any day in her life.

Yet her love swore that this was their last day here. That they'd never be safe in their home again.

Dad set his cup down with a sign. "Alright. Explain what you meant," he told the Shifter. "All of it. Because I'm not going to be run off my land, my home, by some vague threat."

"There is nothing 'vague' about this danger." Only Brandon refused to sit still. He paced their small kitchen. Back and forth, from window to door, over and over again. As if he could walk off the guilt that tormented him. "Remember that we're discussing the man who nearly killed your son."

She wanted to pull him to her, to force him to stop torturing himself for his 'failure.' Somehow, though, she couldn't imagine a Dragon would be happy to have people 'make' him do anything, no matter how good their intentions were. Best to let him deal with his feelings in his own way.

Maybe focusing on the problem would dispel his gloom. "A few hours ago, you said we'd only need to leave for a couple days – just until your Flight arrived. What changed?"

"What *changed* is that I failed you," he snarled.

Hannah winced. Okay, that hadn't helped at all.

He paused in his endless pacing, gripping the kitchen counter with hands that suddenly flashed into black scales and claws. Eyes closed, he rocked back and forth, fighting some silent command from his Dragon. Slowly talons and scales faded. And when he opened his eyes again, he was in control of himself.

"I will try to explain. Everything," he nodded to Dad, "as you requested."

"When I said those things, Hannah, I thought that the Wellspring was nearly dead. LeMar would, of course, desire it. Any sign of magic made it valuable. But in truth there was nothing he could do with a crippled Well. A sufficient show of force – a full Flight of Dragons, for instance – would run him off."

With a gasp, she saw his logic. "But now he knows the Wellspring is fully healthy. Well, not fully… but getting there."

He nodded. "Which, as I have been trying to convey, makes it priceless beyond measure. The first Wellspring to reawaken in centuries. A prize worth dying for. And killing for."

Silence fell as they all considered that. Mom sat, lips pinched, hands closed in a death-grip around her coffee mug. Hannah felt her thoughts scatter like a flock of sparrows. There had to be another way! Something they could do to save her home! But nothing came to her. No plan, no idea, no inspiration. Nothing.

Only Dad remained unpersuaded. "You said you had a 'Flight' of Dragons. I don't know how many that is, but it's a bunch, right?" The Shifter nodded. "Is that not enough? If you need more guys to back you up, can't you call another Flight to help?"

"It isn't a matter of force. My Flight could repulse any direct attack. But our enemy isn't honorable. He'll never face us. What he'll do is what he's done."

"He'll send minions to attack your family, like the Wolves who ran down Danny. Your cattle will be poisoned by Rats. Spells will steal the life of your crops and leave them withering in the fields. And all the while, your enemy will hide, safe in some compound in Europe, Asia, or some tiny island not even on the maps. The loss of pawns will not perturb him. He will harass us, endlessly, seeking to weaken us and break our will with his terrorism. In the hopes that, eventually, he *can* launch a full assault."

One word pierced through the fog of hopelessness that enveloped her. "You said 'us.' Does that mean you'll stay? No matter what LeMar does?"

"Of course!" The question seemed to startle him. "My Flight and I will defend this place with our lives."

"Then there's still hope that…"

"No." Brandon stepped to her side and put his hand on her shoulder. "As I said, we will save the Wellspring. Of that, I have no doubt. But your farm is lost. It will never be safe. It will become an armed camp, the heart of a war. Full of strangers and Shifters. Always shadowed by threat of attack. It will survive… but it will never be a home again. Because of me." Blue lights flickered in his eyes as his Dragon's shame filled him.

Her own eyes glittered too, with tears. "Okay. I… I see your point. And I c-c-can't think of any way to save this place. But please, Brandon, *please*! Don't blame yourself. There was nothing you could have done."

"I could have *killed* him," he growled.

"And after what he did to Danny, nothing would have made me happier!" The venom that filled those words shocked her. She'd never known that she could honestly hate someone. "It wouldn't have changed anything, though! I'm sure he shared the information he gathered. If LeMar died, another member of the Fangs of Apophis would follow up to see what happened."

"Actually, I doubt he told anyone about the Wellspring. The Fangs work together against us... somewhat. However, they are treacherous and untrusting by nature. They have no loyalty, no honor. If he spoke of the Wellspring, a stronger Worm would steal it from him. No," he sighed and shook his head. "I'm sure LeMar fears his 'allies' as much as his enemies. This news would have died with him. I could have saved your home this morning. Now it's too late."

Silence again. Hannah didn't even try to hold back the tears that trickled down her cheeks.

Dad was the first to speak. "So, what now?"

"I strongly suggest that your family leave."

"Today?" Hannah gasped. Surely, he couldn't expect them to simply walk away from their lives without a backwards glance?

"I'm sorry, but every hour you linger puts you at more risk."

"Alright then." Dad rose heavily to his feet, face grim. "Take a half hour. Everyone pack a bag and grab anything you can't live without. I'll run to the bank and..."

"Don't," Brandon interrupted. "I'll see to all expenses. It's the least I can do."

"No!" She leaped to her feet and stared in horror at the

two men. "You can't be serious! There's got to be something…"

"Baby…" The roughness in her father's voice cut her protest short. For the first time, she realized that he, too, was close to tears. "I can't let them hurt you the way they did Danny. I couldn't live with that."

"But this is our home!"

Dad blinked and kept blinking until the last dampness left his eyes. "We're a family. We'll make another home. Now go pack! Time's wasting."

CLOTHES WERE THE EASY PART. SOME JEANS, A SKIRT, A handful of blouses, underwear. Hannah didn't care much about them. As she turned from her closet, though, she spotted her great-grandmother's tarnished silver hand mirror. She couldn't leave it behind!

And what about the old photo albums in the attic? The ones with pictures going all the way back to the 1800s? Or the painting of her grandparents, hanging in the hall? The Christmas tree ornaments she and Danny made when they were young? Her mother's wedding gown, stored away with cedar to protect it from moths?

That was when the true horror hit her, as she wandered through her home. Everything here meant something. Every piece of furniture, every knick-knack told a story. Each one was a piece of her, her history. Choosing between them was like trying to decide which parts of her soul she 'really' wanted.

Her search led her at last to the living room. Brandon stood by the window, staring across the yard at nothing. He turned as she came in.

She ought to say something. Rightly or wrongly, he blamed himself and she knew he must hurt as much as she did. Wrapped in her own pain, however, words failed her. After an awkward pause, Brandon nodded silently and returned to his brooding vigil. She grabbed her parents' wedding picture and turned to leave.

As she did, he spoke. A low murmur that she could barely make out. But what she heard chilled her.

"You were right to reject me."

The photo nearly slipped through her numb fingers. "Brandon, no! I'm not rejecting you! I… I love you! How can you doubt that after everything that's happened? After everything we shared?"

He turned from the window and, for the first time since LeMar's escape, met her gaze fully. "Yet you wish to leave me."

"No, I don't!" Drawn by his pain, his confusion, she drifted closer. "I love you. But I love my family too. You're a Dragon. You *must* understand that I can't abandon them, and my duties, no matter how much I want to run away with you!"

"I'm not asking you to desert your family."

"Yes, you are. Or, well, I thought you were. And I just didn't know what to say. It all happened so suddenly."

His lips pinched, biting back an argument, and she loved him for it. For the fact that, even in the midst of his pain, he fought to be gentle and patient. The soft touch of that love warmed her, lightening – for a moment – the dark cloud that hung over them.

Should she tell him what she suspected? That the passion they shared at the Wellspring had brought the promise of a new future? That she believed she was carrying his child?

No. Not at this dark moment. News like that should be delivered in the midst of joy, not sorrow. For the time, it would remain her secret.

Brandon cleared his throat. "I pray that you feel differently now."

"Well, a lot of those duties don't exist anymore," she admitted. He winced, and immediately she regretted those words. How could she even talk about this without making him feel like he had destroyed her life?

Since, in a way, he had.

Guilt flared at that treacherous thought. But after that brief flash of shame, she saw her error. The events of the last few days hadn't destroyed her life – they'd changed it. She wouldn't trade Brandon's love away, not even to win back her farm. No matter what disasters came, she didn't regret meeting him. Or loving him. As miserable as this moment was, at least *he* was in it. That made it better than anything she'd ever had before.

Maybe one day she'd see the silver lining in this cloud. She'd look back and realize that this catastrophe had freed her, let her devote her life to her Mate. (She could call him that again, without regret.) Maybe the magical powers of the Wellspring would let her to heal her brother. Good things could come from this, things she should feel grateful for.

Not now, though. Now it just hurt too much.

As she struggled to put those feelings into words, Mom slipped in carrying a tray with two Mason jars on it. "The last of the lemonade," she said, handing one glass to each of them. "Drink up."

Hannah just held her jar, but Brandon dutifully took a sip. "Mmm." He ducked his head to her mother. "This is very good. Thank you."

Mom chuckled as she wandered off. "It's plain old lemonade. Nothing special. But I'm glad you like it."

He took another, deeper gulp that proved he wasn't simply being polite. The sight brought a smile to Hannah's own lips. "Thank you." She stroked his arm, fingers light upon its hard muscles.

"For what?"

"For being so kind."

Puzzled, he cocked his head. "What is 'kind' about liking good lemonade?"

"Well, I'm sure you're used to nicer things," she stammered. "Pot roast last night and now lemonade in a Mason jar. It's not like it's a filet and fine wine."

"Hannah!" He put his glass down on the sill and pulled her close. The warmth of his body, his nearness, drove all thought from her mind. "You don't think I look down on your family, do you?"

"It's okay," she said – even though it wasn't. "We're not anything special."

He cupped her chin and tilted her face up, making her meet his gaze. "You don't truly believe that, do you? That the love your family shares is 'nothing special'?"

"No. But the lemonade is, is…"

"Tasty. Made, and offered, with love."

"…in a Mason jar," she muttered.

He rolled his eyes, startling a smile from her. "What does that matter? Though in all seriousness, there is something you need to know if you're going to be a… a Companion of Dragons."

"Dragons love the riches of this world as much as any mortal man. More, perhaps, because our emotions run so deep. But they're traps. When we lose ourselves, our purposes, we become dazzled by wealth. We try to dull our pain with gluttony and greed. Remember all those fairy tales about Dragons sleeping on piles of gold?" He picked his lemonade back up. "That's what happens when we forget ourselves. The day I stop caring about life's simple pleasures is the day I take my first step down the road to the Worms."

Wait. *...the first step...*

Her jaw dropped.

Seeing that, the Dragon grimaced. "Forgive me. I was foolishly poetic over lemonade."

"I know where he is."

"What?" He leaned close to catch her whisper. "Where who is?"

"LeMar. I..." Her voice rose into a delighted shriek. "I know where he is! He's at the inn at Pleasant Pond! If we hurry, we can still stop him!"

Brandon stared at her like she'd gone mad. "How could you possibly know that?"

"Because of the lemonade! Don't you see?" Giddy with delight, she laughed at his confusion. "Because he's him and you're *you*. Would Stephen LeMar drink lemonade out of a jar?"

"I think not."

"Of course, he wouldn't! And I'll tell you what else he wouldn't do. He wouldn't eat at Mack's Diner. He wouldn't grab snacks at the Corner Market or sleep at the Rest-a-While Motel. Don't you see?" In her excitement, she started bouncing from foot to foot. "He's a Worm, not a Dragon. Nothing in Beverly is good enough for him!"

Brandon's face lit up as he saw the direction of her logic. "And the inn at Pleasant Pond...?"

"Is a five-star resort about fifteen miles north of here. It's the only fancy place anywhere near Beverly! I mean, maybe LeMar drives all the way from Sarasota Springs. If so, we're screwed. But he's a *Worm*." She grinned in triumph. "I bet he's lazy. Why go that far when there's someplace closer?"

"Oh, Hannah!" On his lips, her name blossomed into a hymn of praise. He drew her to him, kissed her gently on the forehead. "Oh, my Mate! You are brilliant!" Once more, hope and defiance filled him. The last traces of that self-loathing guilt vanished. He had a chance to atone for this morning's failure and she knew he would die before he 'let her down' again.

To linger, in his arms, basking in his love and admiration… she would give anything to stay here, forever. But their window of opportunity was closing, fast. As fast as a scared Worm could run.

A quick peck on the cheek and she pulled away. "I'll get the keys to the Chevy."

"Hmm. You're right. I should drive rather than fly. Save my strength."

She'd known *that* was coming! "Nope. I'm driving."

"Hannah!" His voice rose, growing deeper, firmer, as it was touched by his Dragon's authority. "You will not accompany me."

Already on her way out the door, she didn't even slow. "Yes, I am. C'mon. We need to get moving."

"I cannot allow you to take such a risk." As if he could stop her! "Besides, there is nothing you can do to harm a Worm."

"I know." Snatching the truck keys from the hall table, she trotted towards the front door. Her Dragon followed her, eyes bright with annoyance. "I gave him both barrels this morning and all it did was make him change his clothes."

"So why risk yourself? Trust me. Let me handle this."

Hannah skidded to a halt, spun, and grabbed Danny's hoodie from the coat rack. She was going to need that. "Because I know the inn and you don't. I cleaned there for a couple summers in high school. C'mon." Slipping on the jacket, she ran for the truck. "Let's discuss this on the way."

Though seething with dissent, he did follow her. Hannah hopped behind the wheel and grabbed Dad's sunglasses hanging on the visors.

As she threw the truck into reverse, Brandon opened his

mouth. She cut him off before he could renew the argument. "How strong are you right now?" She hated the way that made him wince, but he had to be honest. Her home, her life, depended on it. "Can you run LeMar down?"

"I doubt it."

"So, you have to catch him by surprise. Which means you need to know where he is. Can Shifters see each other?"

"Yes," he grumbled. Not liking the direction the conversation flowed.

"That means you can't just walk in there looking for him. I can."

"He knows you too."

She flipped up her hood and slid Dad's sunglass onto her nose. "Ta-da! Pretty cruddy as disguises go, but it'll have to do."

That won her a deep rumble of discontent, which she ignored. "I'll go in. I'll find where he is – whether he's staying at the main lodge or in one of the fancy lakeside 'cabins.' Once I know his location, I'll text you. And then I'll leave. I promise!" She risked a glance at his dark, stormy face. "If all goes well, I won't even see LeMar."

"And if all doesn't go well?"

"Then you'll save me," she grinned. "See? I do trust you!"

It was easy to be brave sitting beside Brandon in the safety of her truck. Now, however, as she strode across the lobby of the inn at Pleasant Pond, Hannah found herself shaking with nervous jitters. A cowardly corner of her mind wished she'd let him handle this, as he wanted. She was a farm girl, not a warrior.

She hushed that doubt. She wasn't just a farm girl – she was also a Dragon's Mate. And she would help her love in any way she could.

The lobby was empty. Not surprising, since it was mid-week in the off season. An official inn at Pleasant Pond sedan idled out front, its oblivious driver texting. The door to the manager's office, behind the front desk, was closed. One young man tended the reception desk. He glanced up as she walked briskly past and her stomach twisted into a knot. Could he tell she didn't belong here? Would he call her out and demand to know what she was doing? Gritting her teeth, she passed him without a sideways look. Only when she reached the edge of the lobby did she risk a peek back.

Despite her casual clothes, her fake confidence must have fooled him because he was once more engrossed with his computer.

Her goal lay just ahead down a corridor to her left: a house phone, exactly where she remembered it. There was no point asking the front desk for LeMar's room number; hotels never gave that information out to strangers. Instead she picked up the phone and pressed the button for reception.

"Hello, front desk? The ice machine on the fourth floor has gone crazy. It's spitting ice everywhere. Unplug it?" Remembering some of the rude people she'd dealt with here, Hannah put on her best snotty voice. "That's *your* job, not mine! And I suggest you *do* your job before someone slips on an ice cube and breaks their neck."

She slammed the receiver down and stepped quickly away, pretending to search for something deep in her pocketbook. Seconds dragged by… a minute. Her jitters doubled. Did the clerk not believe her? Was he calling maintenance instead of fixing it himself? Just when she was about to give up, rapid footsteps echoed down the main hall. A flustered young man jogged past without a single glance in her direction! Hannah waited until she heard the 'ding' of the elevator closing. Then she sprinted back out into the entry.

Still empty! Shivering with excitement and fear, she scampered behind the front desk to the inn's computers. No doubt the password had changed since she worked her, but in summers they often got sloppy and left it scribbled on a sticky-note for the new hires.

She needn't have worried. The poor kid had been so frazzled he ran off without exiting the check-in program! Hannah sent the guy a silent apology as she scanned the list of current guests.

There! Room 312, Main Lodge. Stephen LeMar. Checked in under his own name, no less! Though why shouldn't he be? Not even Brandon knew him personally.

She tabbed to his entry. No address – not that she'd expected one. No license plate for a car. *Tons* of room service. Hannah gulped when she spotted the size of his wine bill. Oh yeah. Total Worm. Nothing but the best for this guy!

Yet even Worms had to pay for their comforts. While the inn might offer the latest luxuries, their computer system was old enough that it still displayed a customer's credit card information. Giddy with triumph, she pulled out her phone and took a quick shot of the numbers beside LeMar's name. If they missed him here, maybe Brandon could use that to track the Worm down.

A note beside that number, though, made her heart drop. "Paid in full."

LeMar had already checked out! They were too late!

"What are you doing, young lady?"

With a squeak of shock, Hannah spun on her heels. Mr. MacFarlane, the inn's manager, stood behind her, fists planted on his hips in outrage. Too late, she remembered how he liked to nap in his office in the afternoon.

"I… I, um…"

Think! she begged herself. *Say something! Anything!*

A con man could have invented a story on the fly. But she was honest – and for her, deceit took a lot of planning.

Before she could even apologize, the manager plucked her phone from her hand. "I saw you taking pictures."

No! That was her only way to warn Brandon! "Give that back!" She snatched at the phone but missed as MacFarlane tucked it in the pocket of his pants.

"I think not!" he snipped, backing into his office away from her. "You'd best leave, right now. I'm calling the police."

With a 'ding', the elevator door slid open. Hannah glanced over, expecting the desk clerk.

What she saw was worse.

Much worse.

Stephen LeMar strode quickly down the hallway, followed by a bellboy struggling with a cart full of luggage.

He hadn't left yet? Of course not – the car outside! Her eyes widened as one piece of the puzzle fell into place. That was his ride to the airport. They could still stop him!

If she could get her phone back.

And if LeMar didn't spot her and snap her neck just to punish Brandon…

Hannah dashed into the manager's office, drawing an outraged squawk from MacFarlane. She lunged at him, desperately trying to grab his clothes. But he scuttled around his desk, brimming with indignation. "Stop this! Stop this right now!" he shrilled.

Dammit! LeMar was already halfway across the lobby. She *had* to alert Brandon, *now*! But how? MacFarlane had a phone on his desk… if she could remember more than half of her Mate's phone number. Should she scream? No, Brandon wasn't far, yet there was no way he could hear her in the woods.

Panic welled in her heart as MacFarlane huffed and blustered. The Worm was going to escape – because of her. Because of her clumsiness.

Then, as fear threatened to overwhelm her, she remembered what Brandon said less than an hour before.

I'm sure LeMar fears his 'allies' as much as his enemies.

That was it. The key.

Ice-cold terror swept over her as a dangerous, insane plan sprang into her mind. Brandon would never consent to it. But he wasn't here to complain.

And it just might work.

Stepping back from the manager, she deliberately turned her back on the door, and upon the murderous monster beyond it. Hannah drew a deep, shaky breath – and shouted at the top of her lungs, "Fool! I am a servant of the Fangs of Apophis. Do you even know what that means?"

Safe on the other side of the desk, MacFarlane squinted at her like she was mad. "What are you blathering about? Get out of my office now before… oh!"

His gaze slid behind her and he froze, his mouth rounded in an 'o' of surprise. Hannah's breath caught in her throat. She knew what the man was seeing even before LeMar's smooth, oily voice hissed behind her.

"So. The Fangs sent a spy to follow me, did they?"

Heart pounding, she refused to turn. She simply stood, soaking in the terror… and the danger… of this threat.

Silk clothes whispered closer, until the Worm nearly breathed down her neck. "Tell me who sent you, O Servant, and I may grant you a painless death."

A terrified gurgle bubbled up from MacFarlane, and he began to murmur, "What? What, what?" over and over again.

LeMar must be Shifting.

Good. That meant the threat was real. Fear and triumph warred inside Hannah.

"Well?"

Now everything depended on his cowardice. If the Worm found a spine, she was dead.

"I said…"

"No one sent me." At that, she turned to face him.

Caught halfway between Worm and human, LeMar was a creature of nightmare. Clawed hands, scales glittering on his cheeks and throat, and a mouth full of fangs. Yet he cringed away when he recognized her, and his eyes darted about the room.

Good. She backed away too, putting the desk between her body and the monster. He was just as cowardly as ever.

That meant she might make it out of here alive.

"Stiles!" he snarled. "How did you know... no, never mind." Seeing the empty lobby, he regained some of his composure. "What suicidal urge brought you here alone?"

"Oh c'mon." The desk wasn't much protection, but she felt her spirit soar at the sight of her enemy's unease. "You know the answer to that."

His slitted eyes narrowed, wary of a trap.

A hard, cold smile spread across Hannah's face as she watched her brother's attacker squirm. "I'm not alone. My Mate's nearby. And he always knows where I am when I'm in danger. Remember?"

Anger gave her courage. To see his fear... to let him know that *she*, Hannah Stiles, brought him down... that was a pleasure worth any risk. Sure, a Worm could shatter this foolish desk in a heartbeat and snap her neck...

But he was a Worm, to the end. Craven.

LeMar spun and bolted for the exit. He tore around the front desk and plowed into his hapless bell boy, sending man and bags flying everywhere.

Half-dazed, Hannah walked out of the office in time to see his last moments.

As the vile Shifter dashed towards his waiting car, her majestic Dragon plummeted to earth, slamming into LeMar with bone shattering force. Black scales flashed in the sun. His head reared back, his lips curled, and she caught sight of six-inch-long, dagger-like fangs. Still alive, LeMar screeched, a thin, reptilian wail. Then her Dragon's head snapped forward, silencing him forever.

Besides her, the bell boy screamed in horror. "Plane crash!" he howled. "Plane crash! Call 9-1-1!"

A plane? How could he be so confused? Then she remembered the delirium that the sight of a Shifter triggered in most people. No doubt the shock of it would scatter all real memories of this day.

Leaving the bell boy to his panic, Hannah stepped out of the inn. Chin up, defiant, she strode to her Mate and laid her hand upon his hot, armored side. Letting him know, with deeds, not words, that she loved him in all his forms.

One day after the fight at the inn, Hannah snuggled against Brandon on the porch swing. The pale morning sun offered little heat, but she couldn't have cared less. Next to him, she had all the warmth she needed.

Danny sprinted past them, leaping into the air to catch a pass from his father.

Danny.

Running again. Playing football.

Hannah basked in the pride that brought her. *She'd* done that. Yesterday evening, Brandon carried Danny out to the Wellspring. The love she felt for her brother was far different from her passion for her Dragon, yet every bit as deep. Once more, the waters of the magical pool answered her call. The last evil LeMar inflicted on the Stiles family was washed away by the spring's power.

"Hannah?"

She loved to hear Brandon say her name. Adored the affection, the desire that always seemed to echo in that word when it passed his lips. "Mmhmm?"

He hesitated. Could her Dragon actually be nervous?!?

"There's something we should discuss, if you are ready. The future. Our future."

A lot had changed since yesterday. Everything, honestly! The thorn-covered path to joy had become an open highway. How had she ever doubted? "I know. I'm sorry…"

"Why?" With that pained question, he pulled away from her. "You can't do this! You can't send me away without explaining why you…"

"No! No, no, no!" She kissed him, silencing him in the gentlest way she knew. When she drew back from the delightful treasure of his lips, she smiled. "I meant I'm sorry for what I said yesterday. I won't send you away. Not now, not ever. You were right. We're Mates."

Bright contentment lit his sapphire eyes. Still, he wouldn't rush her. "Are you certain?"

"Yes. Now that Danny's better, he can help my parents. Like he'd always planned. Even if he couldn't…" She leaned close to whisper in his ear. "…I'd still come with you. I love my family and my home. But I love you too. Leaving you would tear my soul in half."

He stroked her hair, his fingers lingering on the curve of her neck. "You know we'll always be a part of this place. My Flight should arrive over the course of this week. With all of us here, we can keep the Wellspring safe *and* still have time to visit all those places I promised. How does summer on a Greek isle sound to you?"

She squirmed. "Well, um, I may not actually be up for that."

"No?" He chuckled – then grew somber when he saw she wasn't joking. "Have you made plans already?"

"*We* made plans. On that afternoon when we made love." She took his strong hand and placed it upon her stomach. "When I summoned the Wellspring, I… felt something. Inside me. Brandon, I'm pregnant. I'm sure of it."

"A child? Our child?" Love and wonder lit his face – and not a little bit of pride. Brandon kissed her lips then bent low and gave a second kiss to her belly where a new life, a new future, lay.

Tilting her face up to the sun, Hannah gave herself wholly to joy. To a glorious, magical future with him, her Dragon protector.

* * *

Thank you for reading Dragon Protector! If you loved it then we are pretty sure you are going to love the next book in the series, Dragon Aflame!

Click here to get Dragon Aflame on Amazon!

Ok, fine…here is a little preview of Dragon Aflame…

THIS IS HOW IT STARTS. THIS IS ALWAYS HOW IT STARTS.

Tess Everlyn opened her eyes, fighting an overwhelming feeling of déjà vu.

She stood on a tiny island near the shore of a pine-skirted lake. Steel grey sky glowered overhead, turning the pond's water a cold, foreboding black. An icy wind whipped its surface into a froth and made her shiver and pull her leather jacket closer.

Nothing except the wind broke the silence that surrounded her. No sounds of cars, people, music… nothing.

She was alone, standing in thigh-high grass. Staring at the island's one other occupant.

An enormous elm tree, tall and straight, soaring a hundred feet into the air. Not a single leaf graced its branches.

That explains the wind, then. It must be November.

But why did she need to guess that? Why couldn't she remember the date or how she got here?

Because I never do.

She knew that. Knew she'd stood here before, a dozen times, struggling to recall herself. Gently, she probed her own mind. There were some things she did know. Her name. The fact that a flimsy log bridge lay behind her, tying the little isle to the mainland. That if she followed the path beyond it, it would lead her to a log cabin about a half mile from here. Her cabin, with a lawn chair, a cord of wood for the fireplace, and a beat up Harley Davidson hog hidden under a dirty sheet.

Skills bubbled up in her mind. A scattering of languages – English, French, German, Spanish, Russian. She knew how to handle that motorcycle, recalled laws of the road and driving permits. Slowly, other facts swam to the surface. This was the country of America, in the state of Massachusetts. No, this part of Massachusetts had broken away at some point and become... what did they call it now? Maine? Yes, that was it.

Her neighbors....

Like leaves caught in a whirlwind, images swirled up in towering chaos. Her neighbors were the Penobscots, a quiet, courteous tribe who left her gifts of venison in the fall. Or were they lumberjacks; rude, prone to drunken affronts, carelessly leveling the woods around her home? No, nosy tourists, begging her for directions to The Hundred Mile Wilderness... snowmobilers roaring past on machines that first enraged her, then enchanted her with their speed and howling fury.

Tess closed her eyes again and shivered, letting the wind and the silence wash away that mad flurry of memories. She didn't know which of them were true. Maybe they all were.

There was only one thing missing from these memories.

Her.

As the past returned, she recalled places, times... all the debris of a life. But herself? Her lovers, family, friends?

Gone. Completely.

Weirdest thing ever – and yet, it felt natural. That sense of déjà vu settled over her again, like a child's security blanket. Things were as they should be, a part of her mind whispered.

Yeah, right. She wasn't the kind of woman who believed things just because people said them. Not even when the person talking was her.

Her eye spotted some small form at the base of the tree. Kneeling, she pushed aside the grass. Amongst the roots lay twelve stones the size of her hand. Each one contained a primitive drawing of a couple. A princess and a harpist. Two farmers with pitchfork and hoe, like a stick-figure version of American Gothic. A pair of hippies decked in flowers, surrounded by arcs of rainbow color. The ones on the left had faded and sunk halfway into the island's soft earth. The farthest right – the newest? – looked brand new. On it, a shaggy-bearded man drove a motorcycle, while a woman stood on the seat behind him, laughing madly as her long hair blew in the wind.

Is that psycho me? she wondered. *Did I ever do anything that crazy?*

She reached for the stone, but as her hand neared it, a shiver swept over her and the hair on the back of her arm rose.

These stones were dangerous. She knew it in her heart. She should never, ever touch them.

So, of course, she did.

The moment her finger brushed the rock's cold surface, a fire-hose of memories slammed into her.

Michael. The way his beard tickled against her skin as he kissed her. The giddy power she felt, standing on that bike, surrounded by wind and thunder. Knowing that any twitch, any error he made would send her plummeting to the pavement. A stupid, pointless death. Yet she trusted him. With her life. With her love. Until...

Tess threw herself backwards, away from the last thoughts. Drugs, bought and sold. Another woman. And another, and another, until...

She sat in the grass, the taste of bile in her mouth.

Why did I touch that damned stone? I knew it was dangerous.

But she knew the answer to that. Because she made bad choices.

That's my life in five words.

Struggling to her feet, she grimaced at the twelve stones. Apparently, she'd made a lot of bad choices.

In her mind, Michael was growing faint again. Feelings died with him. From a pain as sharp as staring at the sun to a vague ache. She still recalled the life they'd begun together, in a cold, distant way. Like the memories of some sad movie she'd watched once, long ago. A few moments later, even that was gone. Leaving her standing, alone, glaring at the stone.

"Okay. Point taken," she said to nobody. "I don't touch those things again."

So what did she know? She ticked the facts off on her fingers and spoke aloud, just so she didn't feel quite so alone. "I'm Tess Everlyn. I guess I've lived a long time." She prayed that picture of a princess depicted a trip to Disneyland, not some medieval romance. "I have really bad taste in men. Apparently, I come here when it all gets too much and I dump their memories in little stones." She frowned down at the rocks with their crude paintings of past loves. "I don't draw very well."

Now what?

A quick scan of the little island offered no advice. Except for a tree and rocks, it was empty.

Stay here? Nah, that was a daft idea. Her leather jacket and pants looked badass, but they weren't all that warm. Besides, what was the point of sitting on a cold, grassy island, surrounded by your mistakes?

Might as well leave. Cross the worn bridge, see where that path leads. Start living again. Get back on that horse and…

…make more bad choices.

With a sigh, she headed out. Maybe this time would be different. Maybe she'd be smart.

Somehow, she doubted it…

Continue the story in the next Dragon Dreams story, Dragon Aflame, here on Amazon…

www.ingramcontent.com/pod-product-compliance
Lightning Source LLC
Chambersburg PA
CBHW062221150726
47991CB00006B/2386